MW01482049

Winter in the Bunkhouse

Winter in the Bunkhouse

by Helena Linn

Seven Cross Lazy L Productions

Winter in the Bunkhouse
By Helena Linn

Published by

꓾

Seven Cross Lazy L Productions
P.O. Box 308
Big Piney, Wyoming 83113
307-276-3506
helenal@tribcsp.com
http://7cross.marincic.com

ISBN-13: 978-0-9817649-0-0
ISBN 10: 0-9817649-0-8

LCCN: 2008907143

Book and cover design by Sue Sommers, WRWS Design
www.wrwsdesign.com
Cover art by Donny Marincic
www.marincic.com

Edited by Gail M. Kearns
To Press and Beyond
www.topressandbeyond.com

Book production coordinated by To Press and Beyond
Printed in the United States of America

DEDICATION

This book is dedicated to God and my beloved
parents Philip and Elva Marincic, who gave me
life, love, and the great gift of growing up
on a cattle ranch in Wyoming.

CHAPTER ONE

A sob caught in Kate's throat as she knelt between the two caskets that held her husband, David, and their four-month-old son, Jeremy. She suffered knowing she would never hold Jeremy again or feel David's strong arms around her. These thoughts overwhelmed Kate as she struggled for words to say a last goodbye. The smell of damp earth caused her to finally realize that the last barrier between David, Jeremy, and her was about to fall into place. She had known death before but nothing had prepared Kate for these final moments.

Silently, Kate asked God to take care of her husband and son. Then she walked over to her friend Margo who was patiently waiting to escort her from the cemetery.

"I'm ready," Kate said unsteadily.

Margo put a hand on Kate's arm and looked past her friend's shoulder. "I think David's mother and sister are coming to talk to you," she whispered.

Kate turned to see her mother-in-law bearing down on her with Denise trailing behind. She had a fleeting moment of pity for Denise, before Marie Webster stammered, "You . . . you . . . you caused this!"

Kate cringed and took a step back.

The distraught woman jabbed a forefinger at her. "If you had been home where you belonged, my son and grandson would be alive today." Shrugging off Denise's restraining hand, the older woman cried, "This is your fault. I told David he was making a mistake when he married you." She fixed Kate with a piercing glare. "Don't think you're ever going to get anything from this family. You're not part of the Webster family anymore."

Bitter as they were, her words reminded Kate of something she had meant to do. She reached into the pocket of her jacket and brought out a small black box. "Mrs. Webster?" she said, in a steady voice. The older woman had turned to leave and stopped only when Kate added, "I want to give you David's ring."

That brought her around. She took the box, opened it, and stared at the ring inside. Glancing briefly at Kate, she murmured, "Well, thank you." Then she turned away again.

Denise touched Kate's arm with her fingertips. "That was good of you, Kate. It's all she has left of her only son, you know."

"All *she* has left . . . ," Margo said before Denise was out of earshot. "How could they talk to you like that?"

———•———

Later, Kate and Margo sat in a quiet corner of a restaurant that Kate had chosen for lunch. Three fresh pink carnations and several sprigs of greenery in a slender vase were a fine contrast to the white tablecloth. Ordinarily Kate might have commented on such an arrangement. Margo lifted the green cloth napkins out of the stemmed goblets so the waitress could fill their glasses with ice water.

Kate agreed to share an order of chicken salad with Margo. They gave the waitress their order and settled back when Kate despondently slumped in her seat and fought back the grief that gripped her in the moment. "Will it ever get better?" she sighed.

Margo shook her head sadly, knowing it wasn't really a question.

Kate looked at her friend across the table. "You must be wondering what all that was about back at the cemetery."

Margo's eyebrows arched. "Not much can explain how they could be so nasty at a time like this."

"I wish you didn't have to go back to Jackson Hole so soon," Kate said. "Even though I know I'm not very good company right now."

"I was hoping I could stay longer, but duty calls. The hospital is short on staff this time of year and there are a lot of tourists to tend to," Margo said.

"I understand," Kate replied.

"Many people came to offer you their condolences so I know you have friends, but you really could use some support from David's family," Margo said in an attempt to get Kate to open up about what had just gone on with Marie Webster at the cemetery.

Kate braced her chin on one hand and said, "You know, Margo, opposites do attract. Look at us. You with your short blond hair and blue eyes, me with . . ."

Margo took up the words quickly, "Long, thick curly hair, brown like your eyes. Tall and slender with a figure to die for." She cringed. "I'm so sorry, Kate."

"It's okay. I've done the same thing myself. Put my foot in my mouth more than once, for sure."

"That's another thing, you are so practical and I'm so impulsive."

"Now, don't put yourself down. I'm shy and you're outgoing and always so cheerful. Maybe it's because we're so different that we enjoy each other's company."

"And you're awfully serious. I worry about how you're going to handle all this grief. I hope you don't bottle it up."

"Don't worry, I won't. I just have to get through it."

The waitress served their food. After a few bites, Margo caught Kate's eye. "Look, we're thirty-two years old and we've been good friends from the day we started nursing school together. It's time you quit changing the subject and tell me why you reacted the way you did to Mrs. Webster's accusations."

Kate kept silent while considering how to respond.

"How can you be so calm?" Margo asked. "I wanted to scratch her eyes out!"

Kate closed her eyes and let out a sigh.

Margo prodded, "She's been mean to you before, hasn't she?"

"I'll never forget the first time I met David's mother," Kate began slowly. "He took me home to meet his parents—he wanted to tell them we were getting married. When he introduced me as his fiancée, his mother's mouth dropped open and she began shouting, 'Fiancée! David! What about Cynthia? You were going to marry Cynthia!' David tightened his arm around me and said, 'No, Mother. You were going to marry me off to Cynthia. I'm going to marry Kate.' Then he told her where and when the wedding would take place."

"It seems Mrs. Webster intended to be in control of David's future," Margo commented.

"I thought she was going to have a stroke when he told her he was joining the Catholic Church and the wedding would be in a Catholic church in Denver."

"I take it she doesn't like Catholics?"

"No, she doesn't," Kate replied. "It was very hard for her to accept that the son she doted on would go against her wishes. It didn't help matters when David's father gave us his blessing and assured him that his decision to join the Catholic Church was fine too." She smiled. "Of course you know that Dr. Webster asked David to join him in his practice in Kansas City and that we moved here right after David's graduation from medical school and our wedding." She picked up her coffee cup, realized it was nearly empty, and set it back down. "David's mother seldom included us in her social affairs and that suited us fine. We stayed busy with our work, had dinner out now and then, and attended concerts when we could—until Jeremy came along." Her eyes lit up and she added with a grin, "Then it was not much sleep and a lot of laundry to do."

Margo motioned to the waitress to bring more coffee and the check.

"Dr. Webster died just before Jeremy was born," Kate continued. "He would have loved his grandson and would have come to Jeremy's baptism if he'd been alive. David's mother reluctantly came with Denise. David's other sister, Carly, was out of town or I'm sure she would have come. She and I have always been friends. Carly and her husband live in Europe now. Denise, sad to say, is so cowed by her mother that she doesn't dare stand up to her."

"Yes, I could see that," said Margo.

Kate picked at her food. "I told Mrs. Webster how important it was to me that the funeral take place in our church. She just threw up her hands and wailed, 'Have it your way. At least this is the last time you'll have things your way.'"

"Kate, you mentioned that David had called from the hospital and asked you to work the evening shift in the emergency room because the nurse had gotten sick. When you said you would, he told you he would be home to take you to the hospital in time for the shift change and then he would take the baby to see his mother."

"Yes, that's what happened."

"Well, why didn't you explain that to your mother-in-law? At the cemetery, she accused you of neglecting your baby and blamed you for causing their deaths."

"I did explain the whole thing to her. I should say, I tried to tell her, but she just wouldn't listen." Kate steadied her voice. "It was the first time I'd been away from Jeremy for more than a couple of hours because I was nursing him. That afternoon, I nursed Jeremy and prepared a couple of formula bottles so we were ready when David came to get us. I was excited about working again, even for one shift." She drew in a deep breath. "Of course, I've regretted that decision ever since."

"You couldn't have known," Margo said softly.

"David's mother never forgave me for taking David away— from her and from Cynthia. She told David he had married beneath himself and their social class." Kate sat quietly for a moment. "Bless his heart, he hated her arrogance but he was never disrespectful to his mother. Carly is a lot like him."

"You've suffered so much." They sat, lost in their own thoughts for a few minutes. At last, Margo said, "And after all that, you gave her David's ring."

"His father and mother gave him that diamond and ruby ring the day he became a doctor. There's no one to leave it to now." Kate put her napkin beside her plate and said, "Shall we go?"

———•———

Early the next morning, Kate drove Margo to the airport. "I hate to leave you like this. You are so alone here," Margo said.

"I know. But I'll be fine, really. There's nothing for me in Kansas City now. I wish I didn't have to leave David and Jeremy here, but as soon as I can sell the house and take care of my affairs, I'm going back to Denver."

"And you will think about applying for a nursing position at St. John's? You can share my apartment, we can visit Yellowstone, ski in the winter . . ."

"Yes, I'll think about it. I've never been to Jackson but I love Wyoming."

"Oh dear, they're calling my flight," said Margo.

"Thank you for being here with me, Margo. I don't know what I would have done without you."

They hugged each other tightly and wiped away tears as they whispered their goodbyes.

During the sleepless night Kate spent after Margo left for Jackson, she made up her mind that she would move from Kansas City and Marie Webster even before the house was sold if she had to. Even though her first thought was to return to Denver where she grew up, she knew she would rather go to Wyoming. Margo had encouraged her to consider working in Jackson. Of course, Wyoming didn't mean going back to the Orland Ranch where she had spent the carefree summers of her childhood with her beloved grandparents. Her heart ached with all the sad memories—of her sixteenth birthday on the ranch, her mother filing for a divorce and leaving two weeks later, and then Grandpa dying so soon afterward. Kate's grandmother hated selling the ranch and moving to Denver but she really didn't have much choice. For Kate, it had been special to have Grandma with her and her dad those few years. She would always treasure the time she'd had with both her grandparents. How she loved their ranch, and how she still harbored a grudge toward Jake McClary for ruining her last day there.

Chapter Two

Four months later, Kate arrived in Denver with the few things she thought she might need to start a new life stowed in her Buick. Anxious as she had been to leave Kansas City, she hadn't counted on the legal technicalities of disposing of all her property. Through eyes blurred with tears, she found and packed away the treasured mementos and pictures of her life with David and Jeremy that she would take with her. Clothes went to the good will center and household furnishings stayed with the house.

Kate had experienced several deaths before her marriage and knew the importance of having wills, but when she and David had theirs drawn up when he was preparing to go to South America the first time, she had no idea she would need his so soon. Getting their house and property into her name so she could sell everything took a lot of time and attention to details. That and dealing with the insurance companies kept her exhausted and emotionally drained. She could hardly believe that the drunk driver's insurance company would look for any excuse to keep from paying for that accident when the police report clearly stated the facts of that boy's fault. She'd had to purchase a new car two days after the accident, and that was stressful in itself. David's partner in his medical practice eased her mind about that property when he asked to buy David's share and promptly negotiated the sale.

When she reached Denver, she found a motel in the suburb where she had grown up. After a few days of rest and walking or sitting in the nearby park, her first order of business was to meet with her accountant.

After embracing Kate and offering his condolences, her father's old friend Cameron Wyatt ushered her to the leather armchair across the mahogany desk from him. He asked a few questions about the sale of her house and the insurance money she had expressed interest in investing.

When they were finished, Cameron closed the portfolio file. "I think everything is in order," he said. "We've pretty well followed the investment strategy we worked out after your grandmother passed away. And the money you took out to buy your house was a good investment. You and David were wise to make the improvements you did and it paid off. I can hardly believe you were able to sell it for so much more than you'd paid for it."

"Good thing we bought into an area that soon developed into a cluster of better homes. Since we had extra building lots, the developer wanted to buy them. I was able to sell them separately and the house sold a couple of days after I listed it."

Cameron picked up a pen and rolled it in his fingers during a few moments of silence. His brow furrowed and he chewed on his lower lip. "Kate," he drew in his breath and went on, "I've known you all your life, and you've endured a lot—your folks' divorce, your dad's fatal heart attack, losing your grandparents—and now this."

Kate closed her eyes briefly. When she opened them, her lips tightened and she blinked several times to hold back the tears. She knew if she looked at Cameron she would break down so she stared at the ceiling until she regained her composure.

"Frankly, I'm worried about you," Cameron continued, "I know you are secure financially. Everyone you've lost has left you money and it's made you quite wealthy. But . . ."

"Cameron, you needn't worry," Kate cut in. "I'm not ready to settle down to anything right now so these plans I've told you about are just for the next few weeks or months." Her voice steadied as she spoke. "If I like Jackson, maybe I'll try to work in the hospital there. At least I'll be with Margo. I couldn't ask for a better friend."

"Well, I just want you to stay in touch so Jean and I know how you're doing."

"I'll have to keep in touch. You have all my money," Kate teased.

Cameron smiled at her quick comeback.

"And thank goodness for that," she continued. "I'm taking enough to manage through several months, and since everything else is invested and we're having all the reports sent to you, you'll be the first to know when I want to buy any property."

Cameron stood up with Kate. Coming around to see her to the door, he put an arm around her shoulders. "I hope you're taking warm clothes. It gets cold in Wyoming."

"Oh, I'm ready. I used to ski. Remember the time you went skiing with Dad and me?"

Cameron laughed. "Sure, I remember. I fell down too many times that day to forget. James didn't take much time off for anything else but he sure liked skiing." He added, "I still miss him."

"I do too." She swallowed hard. "He would have loved Jeremy."

"I know," Cameron said softly.

She told Cameron goodbye and promised to call when she reached Jackson.

On the way to the parking lot, Kate stopped at a newsstand and picked up a copy of *The Denver Post*. She looked at the date—November 5, 1957—exactly four months had gone by since the worst day of her life.

After soup and a sandwich at a coffee shop near her motel, she propped herself up on the bed in her motel room and read the newspaper. When she finished, she went over the map again. She reassured herself that several hours of driving and an overnight stay in Riverton or Lander would give her a chance to drive by her grandparents' old place the next morning. Although nothing seemed exciting at the moment, the prospect of seeing their ranch again was comforting. She expected there might be some snowy roads, but the weather report seemed favorable so most likely the road to their place would be passable. Besides, there was no need to hurry; she hadn't told Margo exactly when she would be in Jackson.

As she did every night, Kate wept with loneliness, said her prayers, and reminded herself she was blessed to have had David and Jeremy even for such a short time. As an emergency room nurse, she had seen the pain and suffering of her patients and their loved ones again and again, but now the pain and suffering were her own. The image of seeing David and Jeremy on stretchers in the emergency room, their lives draining away, haunted her day and night.

She awoke the next morning anticipating her trip to Jackson; she glanced at the clock to make sure she wouldn't be late for daily Mass in St. Matthew's Church where she and David had married. Kate put on her forest green woolen pants, a long-sleeved cotton shirtwaist blouse, and a matching sweater, and then checked out of the motel.

Even though she was anxious to be on her way to Jackson, Kate was glad to see Mrs. Carson at Mass. The elderly lady and Kate's grandmother had become good friends during the time Grandma Orland had lived with Kate in Denver. Mrs. Carson suggested they go to a coffee shop nearby.

When they were seated and had ordered coffee and toast, Mrs. Carson told Kate that things hadn't changed much for her. She was fortunate to live nearby the church because she didn't drive anymore. The priest Kate knew had died two years ago and they really liked the young Irish Father Murphy who took his place. Her daughter had recently moved back to Denver and she was enjoying having her grandchildren close by. She hated to think about winter coming.

Kate listened quietly until Mrs. Carson turned her attention to her young friend. "My dear, you haven't told me why you're here. Are you alone?"

Kate toyed with her coffee cup. "You probably don't know that David and I had a son, Jeremy. He was born last March."

"How delightful for you."

"The rest of my news is not very happy," said Kate.

The elderly woman's smile faded and an anxious look came over her face.

"David and Jeremy were killed in an accident in July."

"Oh, my dear, I'm so sorry."

Neither spoke for a few moments. Mrs. Carson covered Kate's hand with her own and said, "They are with God, you know, and your grandma, and your dad too. I'll have some masses said for them."

"Thank you, I appreciate that."

Kate drove her friend home and said goodbye at the door of a small brick house. As she drove away, Kate decided a late departure was of little consequence in light of the visit with her grandma's old friend. The idea of seeing her grandparents' ranch home again had already lifted her spirits but now she felt quite lighthearted. She reminded herself that it wouldn't be the same; the ranch had been sold to the McClary family and Kate had never quite reconciled herself to the fact that she no longer belonged there.

Kate began to relax a little after she left Cheyenne and all the heavy traffic between the Colorado and Wyoming capital cities. Out in the country there were fewer radio stations to choose from. Maybe someday she could be captivated by Pat Boone's "Love Letters in the Sand" or "Bye Bye Love" by the Everly Brothers and other songs about love, but right now she was glad to find a station that featured Elvis, Jerry Lee Lewis, and music that enlivened her long drive. She found herself listening to Johnny Mathis, Ricky Nelson, and other popular artists, before she caught a western station where she sang along with Marty Robbins on "A White Sport Coat" and harmonized with Hank Williams on "Your Cheatin' Heart." When "I'm So Lonesome I Could Cry," another Hank Williams hit came on, it felt like he was singing directly to her.

Before she reached Casper, Kate had seen mountains in the distance and lots of sagebrush up close. After a short break for gas and coffee, she set out on the road to Shoshoni where all she could see were hills and more sagebrush. She laughed when she remembered what her grandmother often told people. "In Wyoming, it's a hundred miles to anywhere." Kate said to herself, "You were so right, Grandma."

Deciding she'd driven far enough for one day, Kate checked into a hotel in Riverton, had an early dinner, and walked up and down Main Street until the sun set and the day lost its warmth. The next morning she was awake in time to begin the clear, chilly day with daily Mass and a hearty breakfast that would see her through to a late lunch somewhere along the road to Jackson. As a precaution, she found a little store, bought a few snacks, and filled her coffee thermos, thinking again of the long distances between Wyoming towns.

About twenty miles out from Lander, Kate pulled onto a scenic overlook where she could experience the awesome view of Red Canyon. Kate remembered standing with her grandfather on this spot to study the rolling hillside on the left, and then they would turn toward the craggy bluffs on the right that dropped off into a canyon far below the highway. Only the red of the bluffs showed now because snow covered the hillside and ranchland at the bottom of the canyon, but Kate knew that when the snow was gone one could see the red dirt and know why it was called Red Canyon.

After standing there for some time, lost in thought, and getting chilled to the bone by a brisk breeze, Kate slid back into the warm car and checked the clock on the dash. Five past ten—plenty of time to get to Jackson in the afternoon, she decided, even with an excursion into the ranch. A cup of hot coffee and the car's heater soon had her warm and anxious to be on her way again. She and her parents had gone over South Pass during the early fall and late spring a few times, and she remembered how her grandparents would caution them about driving that stretch if it was stormy. She decided that the sky with bright sunshine and a few cumulus clouds, flat and gray on the underside and all fluffy above, hardly seemed threatening. They were off toward the mountains anyway. There was a little snow on the road, but so far it hadn't been slick. Certainly nothing to worry about, she thought confidently. Snow was four or five inches deep on the west side of South Pass, but she was relieved when she reached the turn-off to her grandparents' ranch just past the Sweetwater River bridge. The dirt road hadn't been plowed but it had been well traveled and the snow was packed down. Kate assured herself that she could turn around if there was more snow farther on. And even though she didn't remember exactly how far it was into the ranch, which lay in a valley along the foothills of the Wind River Mountains, she figured it had to be at least forty miles. She'd only been there in the summertime or early fall, and her grandparents had always been snowed in for several months of the year so there could be more snow on down the road. But by now she was intent on making the journey.

Farther along the way, she realized she had only a vague recollection of the road and terrain because someone else had always driven to the ranch. But she was sure it was the right road leading to the place where her days had been carefree, where she could ride the horse her grandpa had given her, and where sometimes he would take her fishing.

Her memories, however, were not all pleasant. Everyone at the ranch had been worried about her grandfather's failing health that summer, and her last day on the ranch had been disastrous. She had been with her grandparents since school let out that spring. Then when Grandpa's horse fell with him and the severe break of his thighbone left him bedridden, Kate's father immediately arranged to be away from his business for a few weeks to be with his parents and help out at the ranch. Kate's mother went along, even though she seldom wanted to go to the ranch. To this day, Kate still wished that her mother hadn't gone and that her dad hadn't tried to help with the haying.

Although she had never let her dad know, Kate had always resented her father's lack of interest in the ranch and the fact that they didn't live there. She loved ranch life and always thought how disappointing it must have been for her grandparents that their only son would never take over the ranch. But that summer Kate saw how much her father suffered with allergies and she began to understand why he chose a way of life that spared him such misery. What's more, her father, James, had married Lillian, a woman with no interest in anything or anybody that didn't center on her own desires. It was inconceivable to Kate that a wife who required a cleaning woman to come in twice a week would have even known how to do the work on a ranch. During the three weeks they spent at the ranch that summer of 1941, Lillian had proven she wasn't cut out for ranch life. She treated it like a vacation and did very little to help her mother-in-law with the work. Grandma had extra hay hands, a sick husband, James, Lillian, and Kate to cook and clean for, but Lillian spent most of her time reading and taking walks. The divorce came about soon after their last day at the ranch. On that day, Kate had approached her parents' bedroom door to tell them about her broken arm, but the angry words being exchanged by her parents stopped her from interrupting them. She had overheard enough to know that her father was berating her mother for not helping his overburdened mother.

Kate's broken arm made it necessary for them to leave the ranch without delay. Lillian Orland was out of their lives soon afterwards, but not before she got a generous settlement. Kate's attempts to locate her mother to tell her about David and the birth of their son met with no response. Kate finally confided in David that she'd overheard her mother tell her father that since he was the one who had wanted a child, she didn't want to share custody or any responsibility for the brat. "So why," she'd told David sadly, "would she care about a grandchild?"

Memories kept flashing through Kate's mind but she was careful to keep her eyes on the snow-packed road. She scarcely realized that the prairie was stark white except for outcroppings of rock and the tips of sagebrush. As a young girl, she'd been fascinated by scrub brush and small trees that seemed to grow out of boulders scattered all over the hillsides. She used to wonder why she couldn't see the majestic Wind River Mountains as she drove to the ranch. But now, she realized, the road was so close to the mountains that the foothills obscured the peaks behind.

The road dipped to a low place where a bridge spanned a dry creek bed. It was a gradual climb to flat land where the road wound around for several miles until the tracks rose to the top of a hill. Approaching the hilltop, Kate kept to the right side as much as she dared. She knew the ridge could easily pull her car into the snow if she got too close, but nothing prepared her for the sudden appearance of a pickup as she reached the top. With inches to spare, both drivers managed to pass each other but the drop on the other side caught Kate unaware and she automatically put her foot on the brake. The car began to spin and seconds later it stopped with a jolt. Kate sat stunned in a tilted position with the back end of her car downward in the ditch.

She waited until her adrenaline receded, leaving her feeling weak, then opened the door and stepped down into a foot of snow. With some effort, she clambered to the roadbed to assess her situation. She got back into the car and after a few attempts to drive out of the ditch, with the tires spinning in place, her suspicions were confirmed. The car was stuck. Maybe coming here wasn't such a good idea. Within minutes, she figured it wasn't only a bad idea, but it might prove awfully dangerous as well if she didn't get out soon.

 CHAPTER THREE

Kate dug around in the packages in the back seat and took out her snow boots, mittens, and parka. Putting them on at a tilted angle and in such a confined area left her exhausted. She shut the car off. Even though the gas tank was nearly full, even that might not last until help turned up, if help turned up at all.

It was slow going but Kate managed to clear most of the snow in front of the tires by using a saucepan she'd packed for the trip. On her knees, she sank back into the snow. She was tired, her arms ached, and she wasn't feeling very optimistic about her car being able to climb out of the ditch. Kate had heard once that some sand, pieces of flat wood, or even the car's floor mats might help with traction. Sand was out of the question, but she caught sight of some sagebrush. *Just the thing.* Luckily, she had a good-sized pocketknife in the glove compartment because she wasn't able to pull the brush out of the ground or break off any of the tough twigs. Her dad had always insisted that she keep a pocketknife, flashlight, blanket, car chains, and a few nutritious snacks in her car, along with a small shovel. She had discarded the shovel and chains while she was living in the city and now she could kick herself for doing that. She bent to cut a sturdy piece of the twisted wood. She gathered a sorry looking pile of the tough sagebrush, placed it under two of her tires, and used her floor mats for the other two. It was all for nothing; the tires spun sagebrush and mats into the snow and the car didn't budge an inch. Disheartened, she got back into the car, turned on the engine again, and worried that the pickup she'd seen might be the only car or truck to pass by until morning. She prayed for help and started to cry.

As she began to warm up, she felt a fierce headache coming on and her stomach became queasy. Right away she suspected carbon monoxide and groped for the key in the ignition to switch off the engine. Opening the car door, she forced her legs and arms to work until she was out of the car and collapsed in the snow. She took deep breaths of the fresh air and tramped to the other side of the car and pushed away enough snow to open another door.

While the car aired out, Kate walked a couple of hundred yards to a bend in the road. There were no cars in sight and no ranch house either. She had no idea how far it might be to her grandparents' place. She headed back to her car. The road wasn't steep and although her car was at the bottom of the incline she wondered if anyone would see it in time to stop, so she walked to the top of the hill where she'd narrowly escaped the collision. As far as her eye could see, there was just emptiness. Kate decided to warn anyone who might come up the hill that she and her car were on the other side. By the time she rummaged through her things and found a red scarf she could tie to some large sagebrush at the crest of the hill, she was worn out and shivering.

The first rule Kate ever learned about being stranded was to stay in the car, and she knew that was her only option. She shut the car doors and wrapped herself in a woolen blanket. When her hands were warm enough, she poured herself a cup of coffee from her thermos. The hot liquid went a long way to warming her up on the inside. Praying fervently, she tugged the blanket more snugly around her body as she tried to shut out the cold that seeped in around the doors, and she scolded herself for getting into such a predicament.

Needing more warmth, she trudged through the snow again and opened the trunk of her car to get out a new blanket and a pillow. She made herself more comfortable but the excursion to the back of the car had chilled her through once more. Checking her watch for what seemed like the hundredth time, she saw that it was four forty-five. Already the sky was showing signs of darkness and she started to feel panicky again. What alarmed her even more were the heavy gray clouds in the west that were moving toward her. The first few snowflakes breezed past her windshield but before long they began to stick, and soon the only light, dim as it was, shone through her side windows. The frigid air continued to seep in around the door. No matter how tightly she pulled the blankets around herself, Kate shivered from the cold. It was impossible to clear the exhaust pipe, so starting the car again was out of the question.

So far, she'd held her worst fears at bay. She had been busy trying to free the car, then too tired to think clearly, but now with darkness coming on, Kate began to realize that she might freeze to death during the night. Strange, she thought, how many times she'd wished she could have died along with David and Jeremy and now that she could possibly die, she knew she wanted desperately to live. She could have died if she hadn't recognized that it was carbon monoxide that had been making her sick to her stomach. She recalled the time when two distraught parents brought their children into the emergency room and it wound up that exhaust fumes had been leaking into their car. Kate's thoughts turned to Jeremy dying in her arms in the same emergency room. The pain and loneliness intensified with the fading light as she curled up in a fetal position, her emotions spent. Kate prayed aloud that someone would come in time. Her slurred words made it hard for her to concentrate on what she was saying. *I can't go to sleep, I'll get hypothermia.* So she forced herself to stay awake by praying louder. It occurred to her that she should leave her lights on just in case someone came over that hill before the battery ran out. She tried to reach the light switch but it was too much effort and she fell back. The dome light would use less battery power anyway so she fumbled until she found the switch and turned it on, discovering that the dim light was strangely comforting. She could even see the clock on the dash—*seven thirty*, she thought, drowsily.

Several times, Kate managed to rouse herself from the overpowering longing to doze off, knowing it could be fatal. After about twenty minutes she could no longer resist the urge to fall asleep. At that moment a vehicle's lights began illuminating the bushes at the top of the hill, but she was sound asleep.

 **CHAPTER FOUR**

Jake McClary had just told Charlie Grady that they weren't getting back any too soon, because the snow was really piling up. They were nearing the top of the hill when he said, "Hey, Charlie, do you see that red flag? What do you suppose . . . ?" They topped the hill and simultaneously both men saw Kate's car in the ditch. By the time Jake had his truck stopped, they'd passed the car so he immediately reversed until they had lights shining on the left door of the snow-covered vehicle. Charlie was out his door first and had to give the frozen door a good yank to pull it open.

"We've got to get 'im out of here," Charlie shouted. Jake had reached the other side when Charlie called out to warn him, "He's leaning against that door," but Jake had already opened the door.

"Open the truck door and we'll get him into the cab," Jake yelled, pulling Kate out of the car.

Kate moaned and tried to lift up her head.

"I'll be darned, it's a woman," Jake said as he settled Kate on the seat of the warm cab.

Charlie got in on the other side and tried to wake her.

"I'll see what to do about this car," Jake said.

After a few minutes, Jake was back at the driver's side of the truck. "It's really stuck but we'll give it a try. Drive up a ways after I get the chain from behind the seat and we'll see if you can pull it out," he instructed Charlie.

Charlie motioned okay.

Jake pulled the chain out of the cab. "Is she awake at all?" he asked.

"Moaned a few times but hasn't said anything."

When the chain was hooked to both vehicles, Jake told Charlie to proceed slowly when he saw the lights come on in the car. When Jake turned on the lights, Charlie pulled the chain taut, and then with steady power he brought the car onto the road. Jake unhooked the chain from both vehicles and said, "Take her on. I'll have to follow in your tracks to get this car through."

Jake was thinking fast—whoever it was they had rescued had a full tank of gas and she hadn't been running the car. *Smart girl*, he thought as he jumped out and cleared the exhaust pipe of the compacted snow and dirt. Careful to stay in the pickup's tracks, Jake managed to keep the car moving. Three quarters of an hour later, he glided through the garage door that Charlie had opened for him.

"Good thing you opened that door. I'd never have gotten going again if I'd had to stop," Jake said, opening the door of the truck to carry Kate into the house. Charlie lit a lamp so they could see and they went on through to a bedroom; Charlie tossed back the covers and Jake laid Kate on the bed. They took off her boots and parka.

"We'd better find something warm to put on her. Maybe Mom left a nightgown in one of these drawers," Jake said, bringing the lamp over to a dresser. He rummaged through a drawer and found a flannel gown.

"Let's get that shirt off," he told Charlie, before slipping the gown over her head. It took both of them a few seconds to get her arms free of the sleeves, after which Jake drew off her jeans as Charlie pulled the gown down to her ankles. "Pretty flimsy underwear for winter," Jake commented with a glance at his sidekick. They pulled the covers over her shivering body. Kate roused enough to turn over and curl into a fetal position.

"Jake, don't we have some heavy socks?" Charlie asked. "Her feet are near froze."

Jake pulled an afghan from the chest at the end of the bed and added it to the blankets covering Kate. He left the room and a few minutes later he came back with a pair of woolen socks.

"You take care of her now," Jake said. "I'll get the fireplace going and bring in the groceries. I'll put the truck away and do the chores."

When Kate heard Jake leave the room she rolled over on her back and brought Charlie into focus. In the dim light, Charlie saw that she was staring at him, with a bewildered and frightened look.

"Oh good, you're awake. Don't you worry any—we'll get you warmed up in no time. I'll bring you some hot tea," Charlie said in his most nonchalant voice. "I'll be back in a jiffy."

When Charlie had the fire going in the kitchen cookstove, he filled the teakettle from the hand pump at the sink and set it over the hottest spot on the stove. He took down a mug and a tea bag from the cupboard. He opened a can of chicken soup and set it on to heat up. By the time he found a hot water bottle, the tea kettle water was hot, so he filled the mug for tea and poured the rest in the hot water bottle. He wrapped it in a thick towel to slip under the covers near Kate's feet.

When he returned to Kate's room, she managed to sit up so he could place a tray with a bowl of soup and a mug of tea on her lap. Charlie stood at the side of the bed. "I'm Charlie Grady and the boss is Jake McClary." Kate tensed up at hearing Jake's name, but Charlie didn't seem to notice. "Good thing we came along when we did," he went on. "Wasn't that you we met at the top of the hill this morning?"

"Yes. I'm Kate . . . Kate Webster." Her voice sounded weak, even to herself.

Charlie pulled up a chair and sat while Kate ate a few bites. He didn't ask questions of her except to inquire if she was getting warm.

Jake took off his coat, cap, and boots in the mudroom. He let his blue heeler dog follow him into the kitchen, and then added more sticks of wood to the kitchen stove.

"Well Buster, are you glad to see us, old boy? Bet you thought you'd been snowed in all by yourself, didn't you?" Jake said, giving the dog a pat on the head. He poured dog food into an enamel pan. Then he picked up a matching pan, carried it to the sink, pumped water to fill it, and set both pans on the floor. Carrying a coal oil lamp, he went to check on Charlie and their unexpected visitor.

"How's she doing?" he asked at the door of Kate's bedroom. Kate was dozing off.

"She's been awake, anyhow. She drank some tea and got down a few spoonfuls of soup." Charlie left the tea and bowl of soup on the bedside table and followed Jake into the kitchen. "Do you think it's okay for her to go to sleep?"

"I'm sure it's okay now, but I imagine she's going to be hurting while she thaws out." Jake gave Charlie one of his disgruntled looks. "I don't like this much. The snow is already deep. We're going to have a job getting that car out of here tomorrow. The snow and wind don't show signs of quitting."

Both men put groceries away in the storeroom and cellar. "The rest can wait till tomorrow," Jake said, closing the door between the storeroom and the kitchen. "It's a good thing we ate in town—I'm ready to hit the hay."

Charlie sat on the stool next to the counter and rubbed his chin. "There wasn't much snow till we got about to the big draw. If we can get her that far, she can probably drive on out on her own." He yawned. "What do you suppose she was doing out there anyway?" Charlie chuckled.

Jake downed a glass of water and looked at his ranchhand. He caught the amused look on Charlie's face. "What's so funny? I don't see anything funny about this situation."

"Oh, I was just thinking, what if . . . what if we can't get that car out. It sure looks like more snow is comin'."

"Cut that out. I don't care how much snow there is. She's getting out of here tomorrow as soon as we have that road plowed." He slammed his glass down on the counter. "Even if we have to go clear to the highway!"

"Don't get all bent out of shape. Just because . . ." He stopped at the glower he was getting from Jake, who left the room without another word.

Charlie decided to check on Kate before he turned in. She was wide awake. "How about a little more of this soup?" he asked.

Kate shook her head no and studied his face a moment. "Did you say your name is Charlie?" she asked. He nodded yes. "Charlie, what I really need to do is to go to the bathroom. Would you mind?"

"Sure," Charlie answered and began to peel back the covers. "Maybe ought to take it slow." He helped Kate to her feet. She took a couple of steps and then reached for the bedpost. Charlie held her arm and waited till she was ready to go on. "Okay, now?"

"Yes, it's just that I hurt all over." Kate managed a smile. "This is a switch. I'm a nurse. I'm not used to being the patient."

With a lamp in one hand and the other under Kate's elbow, Charlie explained that when Jake and his brother Jesse built the house, fixtures were put in for the kitchen and bathroom but they only had cold running water from a cistern. "You can flush the toilet . . . water comes in by gravity. They put in drains so we don't have to throw water out the door. We're sure lucky we don't have to go out in this cold to use the outhouse."

"Boy, I'm glad to hear that," Kate said with a smile.

Kate assured Charlie she could manage by herself at this point and he said he'd wait in the hall until she was ready to go back to the bedroom.

When Kate was settled in bed, Charlie told her he wanted to be sure she was getting warm so he sat on the edge of the bed and chatted with her for a while. He told her that they had managed to get her car out of the ditch and Jake had driven it into the garage. There was an overnight bag they'd brought in, he said.

In spite of her uneasiness about Jake and the anxiety she felt knowing she'd have to face him sooner or later, Kate appreciated Charlie's kindness. Charlie was about medium height and had graying hair that was growing a little thin. His twinkling light blue eyes were steady on her face as he spoke, and he wore the familiar Levi's and a cowboy shirt. She noticed, with amusement, that his forehead was marked where tan and pale met at the hat line, indicating he spent a lot of time outdoors. She guessed he was probably in his fifties.

She sipped her tea but it was quite cool by the time Charlie stopped talking. "I've had enough," she said, handing him the cup. "I'll be fine. Please don't worry about me." She huddled deeper into the blankets. "You've been very kind." Then suddenly she asked, "Would you mind bringing in the big black bag from the back seat of my car? It shouldn't be left out in the cold."

"Not a problem," Charlie answered. "I'll be right back." After he set the bag down, Charlie said, "I'll leave the door open in case you need something. Just holler and I'll hear ya." He crossed the hall and went down into the living room. He put another log on the fire, made sure the screen was in place, and hoped he or Jake would hear Kate if she really did call out for them.

During the night, Charlie woke up and lit a lamp. He checked his Big Ben clock and saw that it was two fifteen. He slipped Levi's over his long johns and padded down the hallway to check on Kate. She appeared to be sleeping soundly so he went back to bed.

———•———

The next morning, Jake and Charlie were at the dining room table eating bacon, eggs, and pancakes when Kate came into the kitchen.

"Good morning," Charlie called out cheerfully. "Come on in, have a chair and I'll get you some coffee." He pushed back his chair and motioned for her to sit to the right of Jake, who sat at the head of the table. "I'll bring you some coffee," he said again. Then he disappeared through the archway toward the woodstove in the kitchen.

Jake, intent on eating his breakfast, uttered, "Good morning."

Kate pulled the chair out and glanced his way, confirming her worst fears and half expecting him to add some derisive remark.

Charlie poured coffee. "Kate, isn't it?"

"Yes, Kate Webster." She smiled at Charlie as he set the mug next to her plate.

Feeling his eyes on her, Kate chanced a glance at Jake.

Jake was studying her face. "Kate? No, you're Kitty . . . Kitty Orland," he said in a clipped tone.

A chill that had nothing to do with her having been caught out in the cold went through Kate. She swallowed hard. "Yes, I'm Kitty but I prefer being called by my name, not that nickname. My married name is Webster."

"Well, Kitty," Jake said, ignoring her words, "just who were you looking for out this way?"

"I wanted to see my grandparents' home again," she said defensively. Surely he didn't think she'd come looking for him.

"Well, you picked a fine time of the year to do that."

Charlie passed Kate the bacon. "I hope you're feeling better. You need to get your strength back."

She gave Charlie a wry smile. "It hurts to warm up about as bad as it does to freeze." She ate a bite of pancake and looked up. "I want to thank both of you. You saved my life."

"Well, it looked like you were only going to need one more clean shirt," Jake remarked. Kate started to grin but sobered quickly when he added in a harsh tone, "I see you've come from Kansas. Surely you know that driving back roads in Wyoming in the wintertime is hazardous business."

"I realize now how foolish it was to get off the highway," Kate responded, without looking his way.

"I suppose you thought you knew where you were going," he said.

Kate swallowed hard. "I studied a map and saw that the road that left the highway back there went on through to . . . Pinedale," she said uncertainly. "I'm on my way to Jackson."

Jake set his coffee cup on his plate and pushed back his chair.

"We have to feed the cattle before we can plow the road. There's stew in the pantry. If you'll heat that up about eleven o'clock, we'll eat as soon as we get in, and then get going as quick as we can."

Charlie finished the last of his coffee and carried his plate to the kitchen.

"I locked the calf in last night so just get enough milk for the pigs and let the calf have the rest," Jake told Charlie. "We don't have time to separate anyway."

Kate followed Charlie into the kitchen and watched him poke several sticks of wood into the stove. "Kate, would you mind keeping the fire going, there's plenty of wood here in the wood box."

"I'll be glad to. Anything else I can do for you while you're gone?"

"The fireplace will need some more logs too. There's magazines and books if you like to read," he said, pointing in the direction of a stack of reading material next to an easy chair in the sunken living room.

Opening the door to the mudroom, Charlie said, "Just put that stew on the back of the stove around eleven—we should get in about noon. You'd better take it easy this morning. You had a close call yesterday. It'll probably take all afternoon to get you to where you can drive out, so rest up."

After Jake and Charlie left, Kate went back to sit at the table. She cupped her hands around the mug of coffee and thought about Jake. *He's changed, older but even more handsome than that summer sixteen years ago. Still has thick curly black hair, thick eyebrows and full dark lashes, the same bright blue eyes. Strong jaw line and chin, firm mouth with even white teeth. About six-foot, muscled with lean hips and broad shoulders. He must be about thirty-seven now. I wonder if he has a wife. But who would have such a beastly man for a husband anyway?*

Kate took a sip of coffee to ward off her irritability. *Of course I've changed too. To think I ever had such a terrible crush on someone as ruthless as Jake McClary. Grandma said Jesse and his family*

*lived here and that Jake was on their mother's old home ranch in
another county. How could I have known he would be here now? I
could so easily have died on that knoll yesterday, but to be rescued by
Jake McClary! Why? Of all people, why him? Grandma had clearly
said that Jake lived on another ranch. Of course, that was eight or
ten years ago,* Kate reasoned.

The Orland ranch was the last one up the east end of the
valley. The McClarys lived almost three miles west of it. Kate
was about eleven when her grandparents learned that Agnes and
Gerald Mortenson, their only close neighbors, were selling their
ranch. The Mortensons were getting on in age, and since both
of their children lived in Arizona they wanted to move closer
to their kids and to where it was warmer in the wintertime.
McClarys, a ranching family from the southern part of the state,
bought the Mortenson property. Grandma and Grandpa Orland
were delighted with their new neighbors. The two ranchers got
along well and helped each other with branding, roundup, and
other work, just like it had always been. Mrs. McClary and
Grandma became good friends and shared many interests. They
were both "born" Catholics and made every effort to go the long
way to town for Mass as often as possible, with or without their
working husbands. During the summer when Kate was at the
ranch, she went with them, as it was assumed she would.

Kate's grandparents had always been her rock. They loved
her unconditionally. She decided long ago that they had quietly
passed on values and given her a sense of self-worth as their
way of helping to shape her character. Her grandma was always
teaching her manners, work ethics, and doctrines and practices
of their faith, along with virtues of honesty and compassion.
And not only to Kate, it was as true for anyone else who came
into her sphere of influence.

The McClary's twin boys, Jake and Jesse, were considered top
hands. Grandma Orland had spoken highly of them on many
occasions. Both boys broke their own horses, they irrigated,
drove teams, moved cows, fixed fence, or whatever needed to

be done. They competed against each other roping calves at the local rodeo but it was good-natured rivalry. They were always alert to when the Orlands needed help and were willing to lend a hand. Jake was more reserved than Jesse but he was never impolite, above all not to the elders around him. Kate knew Jesse better than Jake because it was usually Jesse who came to her grandparents' ranch most often, but that fateful summer it was Jake who came to help with the haying. Both ranches had hired hands, especially during the summer. One in particular had been with the Orlands for years. Kate called him Uncle Ben, and it was he who had to run things when Grandpa got hurt. Ben was mighty glad when the McClarys sent Jake to help with the haying in that summer of 1941. Kate was thrilled, too, because the few times she had seen Jake had been enough for her to develop a teenage crush on him. Jake caught and saddled her horse but only when Grandpa asked him to. She didn't really like it when Jake cajoled her into helping Grandma with the dishes or hinted that she ought to bring the clothes in off the line for her grandmother. But she rationalized every misgiving she had about him because of her infatuation with Jake.

When Kate considered how he had pretended to care for her and then used that pretense to humiliate her, she shuddered to be in Jake McClary's house, having to accept his reluctant hospitality. *Thank goodness I'll be away from here in a few hours. I'll certainly never come this way again.*

Chapter Five

Kate stood at the dining room window and looked out over the ranch yard toward the corrals and the big red barn where Jake was leading a pair of harnessed horses out through the double doors of the barn. He shoved one door along the track to the center of the opening and then moved to the end of the other door and pushed it to the center. She shivered, feeling chilled and raw inside. Pulling her zippered sweatshirt closer around herself, she fought back a dreadful uneasiness that she might have to bear the indignity of another harsh encounter with Jake. She coiled a long strand of her sable brown hair around her finger.

Kate hoped that Jake and Charlie wouldn't be gone long so she could be on her way right after lunch. She even began to rethink working in Jackson. A little over a hundred miles away, the town seemed too close to Jake McClary for Kate's comfort. Kate continued to watch as both horses followed Jake in perfect unison through a gate in the corral. He held their halter ropes in a loose grip. The horses waited for him to close the gate and then resumed their steady plodding toward a hay sled several yards away. One big bay stepped easily over the tongue and stopped, while the other one sidestepped into place on the near side.

The scene reminded Kate of watching her grandfather hitch his favorite team to a wagon. He and Ben would spend half the summer irrigating so the hay would grow, then during August and early September they would cut and stack the hay so they could dig it out of the stack in the winter to feed his cattle. "We have to feed them every single day. The snow is way too deep for them to paw down where they might find some grass," he'd say. The teams they used a lot on wagons or sleds were usually gentle and well-trained, but Grandpa always cautioned Kate to stay out of the way when the men were trying to get the other horses tamed down enough to use on haying equipment. He called it their summer rodeo. He explained that most of the workhorses were only used during haying so they were fairly wild, and it wasn't uncommon to have a few runaways before they got them gentle enough to work.

Kate recalled the summer that the horses had been turned out on the desert for a couple of months to graze before haying season. Grandpa was running horses back in when his saddle horse stepped in a badger hole and caused the bad fall that led to his death later in the season. Ranching was hard work but it was the best life a man could have. Her grandpa Orland said it often and believed it until the day he died. Kate remembered how he would frown and tell her that the hardest part of ranch life was selling calves and old cows that he had raised.

Jake sent a long rein to arch gracefully over the backs of the horses toward Charlie who picked up both reins and climbed onto the sled. Charlie started the horses and Jake sat on the side of the sled until Charlie had driven past the barn and corrals to a gate that led to the east. Jake dropped down off the sled, trudged through fresh snow to open the gate for Charlie, then closed it and climbed back on. They'd gone several hundred yards when Kate went into the kitchen to do the dishes. After she finished, she wiped the countertops and looked around, noting what a good cleaning the whole place could use.

She poured herself another cup of coffee from the blue enamel pot on the stove and went into the living room to sit in a recliner before the fireplace. She cradled the hot mug in her cold hands and watched flames leap from the burning logs. A clear picture of the day Jake deliberately set out to hurt her came to mind.

Kate was in her grandmother's kitchen washing the supper dishes alone when Jake brought his plate and cup in from the dining room.

"Kitty, if I saddle your horse, would you ride part way home with me?" he asked, just above a whisper.

"Sure." She could hardly believe he was asking.

"I'll wait for you by the barn."

Grandma smiled when Kitty told her she wanted to go for a ride with Jake. "Go along, I'll finish up here," she said.

Kitty was out the door and at the barn before Jake had finished saddling her horse. Jake hadn't paid much attention to her until that day. In fact, he hadn't even joined in singing happy birthday to her at the dinner table that evening. As they rode along, he asked her about where she went to school and how long it would be until she graduated. Kitty was astonished but flattered that he was taking such an interest in her. About a mile and a half from the house, Jake pulled up by a grove of aspen and stepped down. "Let's sit on that flat rock for a while," he said, as Kitty got down off her horse.

A breeze rippled the leaves above them. Dry grass and weeds signaled the last of the growing season. The horses, tethered to a low branch, chomped on tall crisp stalks of grass. Jake guided Kitty to the rock and pulled her close beside him.

"You have pretty hair—I'd like to see it out of the ponytail," he said as he pulled off the rubber band and let her hair fall around her shoulders.

"How many more days of haying?" she asked.

He played with a strand of her hair while his arm held her close. "I suppose another ten days or so," he said absently. "How much longer are you going to be at your grandma's place?"

"Not long. I wish I could stay longer."

"That birthday cake we had after supper had a sixteen on it. Are you really sixteen?"

"Sure am."

"Sweet sixteen and never been kissed?" he whispered close to her ear.

Kitty blushed. She really didn't want to admit that she hadn't. But then, when he pulled her even closer, she was sure he was going to kiss her.

"Have you had your birthday spanking today?" Jake teased.

"That's just for kids."

"Not really."

And before she realized his intent, Jake threw her across his lap and held her down.

"Sixteen licks—first one for being a damned nuisance," he said, his open hand landing a smart slap on her buttocks.

"Hey, come on, that's not funny," Kate said, struggling to free herself.

Jake landed another hard smack. "And this is for your dad. A poor excuse for a rancher's son."

The next hit was because her mother was vain and lazy. Another because Kitty followed him around every chance she had and the men were teasing him about it.

When he landed the sixteenth smack, Jake said coldly, "Now, get out of here and leave me alone. I hope I never set eyes on you again!" Roughly, he pushed her off his lap to the ground where she rolled a complete turn. He laughed while she struggled to get to her feet. Kitty felt an awful pain in her arm. Somehow she managed to get back on her horse and start for home.

A log shifted in the fireplace and sparks flew up the chimney. Kate sat up with a start, quite shaken by how she could still be brought so low and humiliated all over again after all these years. She sat quietly for a few moments before taking a sip of the coffee that had cooled and then set the mug on the table beside the chair. The fireplace needed more wood so she put two logs on the grate and picked up her mug. Back in the kitchen she remembered to put more wood in the stove as Charlie had instructed.

Memories of that last day at the ranch, and how upsetting her sixteenth birthday had been, left her feeling disheartened and with a sick feeling in the pit of her stomach, much like the day it happened. Finding herself too restless to read, Kate wandered around the house. She went through the hall at the back of the kitchen and discovered a pantry or storeroom and was amazed that it was so well stocked—enough for a grocery store, she mused. She opened a door on the northeast end of the pantry, which led to a dark and musty-smelling cellar so she quickly shut the door. Looking out the east window of the pantry she could see that the house was built into the hillside on that northeast corner and the hill extended on toward the corrals. In one corner of the pantry a big metal door with a large handle opened to reveal an insulated cooler. She picked up a flashlight on a shelf nearby and peered in. It was as cold as a refrigerator and stocked with bacon, ham, beef, and even chicken, as well as milk, cream, cheese, and butter.

Kate went back into the hallway where it was warmer. She checked out the room off the kitchen where she had seen Charlie go out and found that it was where they took care of the milk. There was a milk separator on a counter and shelves holding milk buckets. The space was being used as a laundry room too; a wringer washing machine and double concrete tubs stood on one wall. There were wooden pegs jutting out from a sturdy piece of planed wood for hanging coats. Above that was a shelf for hats and caps. A narrow cupboard was next to it, and under the coat rack was a long box on the floor for boots. The outside door was on the east and a window next to it provided what light the room needed.

Kate discovered that a roofed porch with a log railing ran along the front of the house, clear to the west end. The west porch was stacked high with logs for the fireplace. With some effort, she leaned over the railing to read what was on the shingle that hung from the roof in front of the living room door. *The Bunkhouse* was carved into the wood. *Odd name for the main house*, she thought.

Shivering in just her sweatshirt and jeans, Kate went back into the kitchen. She decided to take another look at the metal grid she had seen earlier in the hallway. It was quite warm when she leaned down to touch the metal. Must be a gas furnace, she decided. Along the hallway, her bedroom and the bathroom doors were open; near the kitchen another door was open and she could clearly see a single bed, a dresser, and an easy chair with a small table near it. The room between that bedroom and the bathroom had a closed door.

Kate stood on the landing and admired the unique beauty of the sunken living room, especially how the pine railing and newel posts ran along the landing to separate the living room from the hall and dining room. She went down two steps and across to steps going up to the dining room.

Earlier she had seen the outside door in the dining room but hadn't realized it was a Dutch door. Now she found the satiny pine wood and attractive brass fittings absolutely beautiful. She was sure that a window in the upper door was unusual although she'd never seen more than a couple of Dutch doors that she could remember. She lifted the latch to open the top door and was hit by a squall of swirling snow blowing off the roof so she shut it again.

Resigned to the fact that there was nothing she could do about the weather, she went back to the living room and was surprised to see a huge gray cat asleep on one end of a maroon velour-covered sofa.

Someone had cherished the beautiful upright piano near the sofa because it was well cared for. A handsome crucifix hung on the wall next to the front door. Its carved wood was as rustic as a newly fallen tree. An old phonograph stood against the wall on the opposite side of the front door and a few feet beyond it was a large diagonal fireplace in the southwest corner. In the center of the room, there were two brown velour easy chairs and a round glass-covered coffee table made out of a wagon wheel. Two matching gray recliners and a side table between them were placed a few feet in front of the fireplace. Several pictures of horses, hay meadows, and mountains hung on the log walls of the room. She took note of the mantel clock, remembering she had heard it chime several times since her arrival. She supposed that many of the scatter rugs on the hardwood floors throughout the house were homemade. The

Dutch door reminded her of one in her grandfather's barn, though nothing as elaborate as this. She chuckled, thinking how the railings in the room and the Dutch door made her think of a corral and a barn. *Just right for a ranch but this is a pretty elaborate house, especially for two bachelors.*

Kate stoked both of the fires before going over to the piano. An arrangement of photos on top of the instrument caught her eye. There was one of Jake and Jesse, identical twins, in their high school graduation gowns, but the one she studied most was of the two of them in their Air Force uniforms. It brought to mind a letter her grandmother had received from Mrs. McClary telling her that the boys had returned safely from overseas after the war and they would be attending the University of Wyoming that fall. In both pictures, Kate wasn't sure which was Jake, but probably the one who had a serious expression was Jake, and Jesse was the one with a mischievous grin on his face.

Another picture among the photographs was of Jesse, his wife, and their three children—two boys and a girl. Grandma Orland had wanted to attend Jesse's wedding, but she wasn't well enough to go. Kate had shopped for a Pendleton blanket, wrapped it, and mailed it from Grandma to the newlyweds.

Kate lifted the lid from the piano keys and ran her fingers through an octave. Thrilled by the tone of the perfectly tuned old Chickering, she sat down and played "Red River Valley," ended on a trill, and went right into "Have I Told You Lately That I Love You." Tears streamed down her face as she finished the song. It had been a favorite of David's. Most of the time she played by ear but she could read music too and found some sheet music, many with Irish songs and more with western music, in a rack next to the piano. She played song after song, unaware of the passing time until the clock began to strike eleven.

Hurriedly, Kate put the music back in the rack, closed the lid over the keys, and put a log in the fireplace. On her way to the kitchen she stopped to pet the cat, which hadn't moved during her whole performance. She set the pot of stew on the stove, stirred it well, and added two sticks of wood to the fire. Lifting the lid of the coffeepot, she wondered if she should make more but she decided there was too much to throw out. Her grandmother used to make coffee in a blue enamel pot much like this one but Kate had never paid much attention to what she did with what was left. Once the table was set she found a loaf of bread, then opened the cupboard and pulled out some homemade butter. She placed the butter dish on the table alongside the salt and pepper and a sugar bowl. With more time on her hands, she went over to the door and was startled to see fresh snowflakes falling. Visibility on the road was getting bad. Kate hoped that Jake and Charlie would eat fast so she could leave before the road became impassable. In a near panic, she went back and forth from stirring the stew to looking out the dining room windows.

Finally Kate glimpsed the horses coming around some willows. As soon as they disappeared through the barn door, she turned back to fill three glasses with water from the hand pump. Since her grandparents had always had a similar fixture in their kitchen, it seemed quite natural to give the handle a few pumps to draw up icy water. She was sitting at the counter when she heard the men on the porch, stomping snow from their boots.

It was Charlie who greeted her when they came through the kitchen door. "Boy, it feels good to get in here where it's warm." He lifted the lid to the stew. "I'm ready for that, too."

A deep growl caught Kate unaware of the dog that stood menacingly in the mudroom door. She sat very still while Charlie caressed the neck of the mottled blue animal until his soothing voice had calmed the blue heeler. "He doesn't like strangers much but he'll get used to you," Charlie said as he led the wary dog to the back of the stove and poured out some dog food into the pan.

Jake cast a cursory glance Kate's way as he came into the kitchen. Charlie told Kate that they had the truck with the plow on it warming up, then he went off down the hall. Jake dipped a pitcher of warm water from the reservoir of the stove and headed toward the bathroom. A few minutes later he came back, rolling down his sleeves and fastening the snaps of his cowboy shirt cuffs. The sight of his big hands and the flashing memory of how they had whacked her put Kate on edge. Hastily, she moved the pot where the stove was cooler and began ladling stew into two soup bowls for the men and a smaller bowl for her.

Wishing Charlie would return, Kate said uncertainly to Jake, "I don't know what you do about coffee. I've never made coffee this way."

"Well, it's strong but we'll drink it," he said, his words blunt. "We can't take much time anyway. It'll be getting dark before we get you out of here, as it is." He sat down and buttered a piece of the bread.

Charlie was there by the time Kate poured their coffee. Sitting down, she ventured a bite but had to blow on each spoonful before she could put it in her mouth. She took a sip of water and glanced at Charlie.

"I suppose your morning was long. Did you find something to read?" he asked.

Kate swallowed a bite of stew. "Actually, I played the piano most of the time." She looked Jake's way and asked, "I hope that was okay?"

"Mom would be glad you did, I'm sure," he answered, his voice curt. He rose, took his bowl to the kitchen and refilled it. When he returned he reached for Charlie's bowl. "Want some more?"

Charlie handed him the dish. "About half." He looked over at Kate. "Good stew . . . if I do say so myself."

"It's very good. Did you make it?"

"Yeah. We kinda trade off cooking and washing dishes."

Jake came back with Charlie's stew, finished his own meal, and began clearing his dishes off the table. "Don't take time to wash the dishes," he said brusquely. "It's drifting more all the time. Charlie, you take care of the fires and I'll go start her car."

By the time Charlie and Kate reached the garage, Jake had cleared the snow so Charlie could drive Kate's car out and turn it around to follow the plow. Kate got in beside Charlie.

"Jake thinks I'd better drive the car and follow him," Charlie said. "We're sorta used to driving in snow."

"It's fine with me. I'm not anxious to repeat yesterday," Kate replied. They'd gotten only a few hundred yards when the windshield wipers were working at full speed. Kate's anxiety grew every passing second as she tried to see through the fogged-up window. "Why is the snow deeper here than at the house?" she asked, trying to keep the uneasiness out of her voice.

"Well, there's a good windbreak back at the house and we're protected by that and the bluff just northwest of the house. We're out in the open now." Charlie hadn't taken his eyes from the narrow path carved out by the snowplow.

Kate tried to relax but the muscles in her shoulders and neck kept tightening and she had to make a conscious effort not to let Charlie know that she was really worried. She could see that Jake had to stop, back up, and make another run at several of the drifts and they weren't even out of the lane. On top of that, when Charlie stopped the car, it wasn't easy to start moving again. The snow blew across the road causing new drifts to form directly behind the plow.

Kate had been careful not to distract Charlie from his driving by talking much but when she saw Jake step out of the truck and motion them to stop, she blurted out, "Why did he do that?"

Charlie had stopped about fifty yards from the truck. He rolled down the window. Jake leaned in. "It's three thirty and there's no way to get through to the highway. It's snowing and blowing harder than ever so we have to turn back."

Kate's eyes remained glued to the stark white landscape before her.

Charlie explained, "We're at the county road and there's room here for him to clear a space for us to turn around."

"But . . ."

Charlie put a hand on her arm and said, "I know you're disappointed but he's right. We've only come two miles and it's about forty more to the highway."

Kate put one hand over her eyes and shook her head slowly. "Does this mean . . .?" She swallowed hard.

"I'm sure sorry but we're snowed in—could be for several months, I'm afraid."

Kate took a deep breath and let it out between parted lips. Hot tears burned at the back of her eyes. She hardly noticed when Charlie passed Jake's plow and turned around to follow him back to the ranch. The return trip was just as hazardous, and it was a little before five o'clock by the time Charlie drove her car into the garage.

"What do you need to take into the house, Kate?"

She rubbed her forehead, so upset about the turn of events that she could hardly think. Her personal belongings were the last things on her mind.

"Let's just take what you need right now," Charlie said. "We can get the rest in the morning."

"Just those same two cases, I guess," Kate answered woodenly.

Chapter Six

That evening, Kate was relieved when Charlie told her he'd rustle up some supper since Jake had gone to milk the cow and gather the eggs. First he lit two coal oil lamps that were on the counter. He left one there and took the other to the table in the dining room. Trying to be of some help, Kate set the table but thoughts of what was happening to her kept crowding her mind until it was difficult to think what needed to be done next.

As he cooked, Charlie explained that they had cold water come into the pipes from the cistern that was filled from a spring up on the hill, but Margaret McClary had insisted that they keep the pump in the kitchen. "The cistern is on top of the cellar," he said. "Jake and his brother Jesse built this house after the war. They put the house right next to the edge of the hill so they could build a cellar and pipe in water from the spring. The old folks, who had this ranch before the McClarys bought it, lived in that log cabin on the other side of the barn." He handed Kate a loaf of bread and pulled out a breadboard from a lower cupboard. "You could slice some bread for us—there's a bread knife in that wooden holder over there."

"Sure, I'm sorry I'm not much help."

"I guess you've seen the floor furnace but we only leave it on the lowest setting. There's no electricity for a fan, anyway. We'll have enough propane to last the winter but we'd run out if we had a hot water heater so we just use the reservoir on the stove here and heat water as we need it." He pointed toward the mudroom. "There's a boiler on the wall that we use to heat up water for a bath or to do the washing. It takes two to carry it, though. Don't try to do that yourself," Charlie rambled on while he stirred the oatmeal he had cooking.

Kate listened without saying a word.

Charlie put a hand on her arm and told her kindly, "Look, I know this is tough. But we'll take care of you." After a moment, he asked, "Will your family be worried about you?"

"No, my husband and baby were killed in a car accident in Kansas City a few months ago. I really don't have any family. Just a few friends."

Charlie shook his head sadly. "I'm so sorry to hear that. I know what it's like to lose your spouse, but to have your baby die too . . . that must have been a terrible shock."

Kate managed a weak smile. She knew Charlie was trying hard to make things easier for her. She said she couldn't eat anything and excused herself. "I'll be back to clean up after you and Jake have eaten."

Kate sat in front of the fireplace until she heard the men getting up from the table. She was wiping the dishpan dry when both men came into the kitchen.

"Come into the den when you're finished," Jake ordered as Kate was hanging up the dish towel. He disappeared through the door to the hall.

Kate turned to Charlie who was stoking the fire in the kitchen stove. Nervously she asked, "Where is the den?"

"Across the hall next to your bedroom." He lowered his voice and added, "Kate, he's not very happy about this situation, but just remember it's not you."

Kate's eyebrows shot up. "What do you mean?"

"He'd be just as upset if it was any other woman, so like I said, don't take it personal."

But for Kate, it was personal. Charlie didn't know the half of it, so she just excused herself and made her way down the hall.

Jake didn't hear Kate when she first entered the den. She had a moment to observe him, standing on the other side of the room looking out the window of the west wall, his jaw firmly set, and his arms folded in an angry stance.

Bracing herself, Kate drew her sweater edges together and held them crossed over her chest. The room was cold. She approached one of a matching pair of wine colored wingback chairs.

"Sit down," Jake commanded.

Kate ignored his arrogant tone. She didn't need to be told; she wanted to sit down before she crumpled to the floor.

Jake moved to sit in front of a roll-top desk. He swiveled around to face Kate. "This is a hell of a mess. By morning the road will be worse than it is today. The only way out of here till spring is on skis or snowshoes."

"I'm a good skier. Loan me some skis and I'll . . ."

"Didn't you learn anything today?" he cut in quickly. "You escaped with your life once, and unless you've got eight more, you'd better not try something crazy."

His cutting words hurt. She was feeling vulnerable enough without his adding to her misery. The thought of spending months snowbound with Jake was inconceivable but she saw no way out of her predicament. She refused to look at him and kept her eyes fastened on a gray stripe in the braided rug at her feet.

"You'd be lost before you got out onto the main road." His tone softened. "Look, I don't like this any better than you do, but there's not one thing we can do about it. You can earn your keep by cooking and doing the housework."

Kate looked up at him. "I don't see that I have a choice." She cleared her throat and gathered her thoughts. "Mr. McClary, I would like to use your phone in the morning. I need to make two calls."

"That's impossible. We don't have a phone. We have mail once a week . . . you can write letters and I'll take them out to the box before the mailman gets here next Tuesday." Jake glanced at the wide gold band on her left hand. "Your husband may have sent out a search party by then."

"My husband is dead," Kate said tersely, and left the room before he could respond.

———•———

Kate closed her bedroom door and sat on the edge of the bed. Even after all these years, seeing Jake again stirred up painful memories. She had counted on getting away from him without having to deal with any more of their shared past. Now she'd be living under the same roof with him. A helpless longing for the comfort of David's arms around her got her all choked up. She grabbed a pillow and curled into a ball, sick at heart over the situation.

Kate's head hurt, her nose and eyes were swollen and dried out, and she shivered in the icy room. Much as she wanted to pull a blanket over her head to shut out the world, she made herself prepare for bed. She was too spent to follow the usual routine of brushing her hair and applying cold cream to her face. Her grandmother had had some strict rules, and brushing her long lustrous hair one hundred strokes every night was one of them. She was glad that neither Jake nor Charlie was around when she slipped into the hall and made her way to the bathroom. After quickly brushing her teeth, she went back to the bedroom and shut the door, ignoring Charlie's advice from the night before to leave her bedroom door open.

During the night, she woke up flailing her arms. She had been dreaming of Jeremy—of being within reach of him, wanting to pick him up but a set of unfamiliar hands restrained her from touching him. Kate pulled the covers back up and tightened them around herself. She was shaking uncontrollably. It was a minute before she could orient herself in the dark room. The pitch dark brought on more despair and added to the emptiness she always felt after a nightmarish dream had passed.

She got up early and looked around the room. It was the first time she noticed a sick call set with a rosary hanging near it. Grandma Orland had explained to her once what a sick call set was—a crucifix that slips out of the base then stands in a groove of the cross. A priest could use the candles and the holy water stored in the base if he were called to a home where there was a sick or dying person. *Anyone would be dead before a priest could get to this place. What a miserable mess I'm in.* But feeling sorry for herself wasn't typical of Kate. She was determined to change her attitude before going to breakfast so she slipped into the bathroom and splashed cold water on her face. She heard one of the men building up the fire in the kitchen. Patting her face dry and applying cream to help soften the puffiness of her eyes and cheeks, she braced herself for another day of having to face Jake.

In the kitchen Jake was pumping water into the blue enamel coffeepot. Kate made a mental note of how much coffee he poured into the pot before he set it on the hottest part of the stove. "Good morning," she said, ill at ease.

"Mornin'," Jake replied coolly with a quick glance at Kate. "I'll stir up some breakfast. You can set the table," he told her. He sliced bacon from a slab and plopped it into a big cast iron skillet next to the coffeepot.

Kate watched Jake dip a cup of sourdough from a crock and pour it into an oversized measuring cup. He measured out a bit of soda and sugar, poured a little salt into the palm of his hand and added it to the cup. Then he cracked an egg into the mixture. By the time he had the batter all mixed together, the coffee was beginning to boil. He poured about half a cup of cold water into the coffee and moved the pot to a cooler space on the stove. He turned the bacon and pulled a pancake griddle to the hottest surface. Kate was fascinated by the dexterity of his movements.

Into the uneasy silence, Jake spoke just loud enough for her to hear, "I'm sorry I spoke that way about your husband."

"It's all right, you didn't know."

"There's some orange juice in the storeroom. Just go through that door across the hall. There's a cooler with a big metal door."

Kate heard the outside door open and close just as she finished setting the table.

Jake nodded his head toward the door to the mudroom and said, "Charlie will be putting the separator together. You better go see how it's done."

Knowing he couldn't see her, Kate saluted and gritted her teeth to bite back a "yes sir!"

Charlie looked up from taking off his boots. "Good morning," he said cheerily. "How'd you sleep? Enough blankets?"

"Yes, thanks to you. I want to watch how you do the separator."

"Well, it's not too hard, once you learn how it goes together." He took a piece out of a big metal bowl and set it in a bracket fastened to the tabletop next to the separator. "Give this piece a twist and it fits right snug. This rubber ring goes down in this groove." He reached up to a nail on the wall and took down a metal hanger that held about a dozen disks. Clasping the disks in one hand he pulled the rod out of the hanger. "These slip right over this shaft with the slots, this piece goes on next, and then the lid. You screw it all down with this wrench and put it in the separator, then set this piece on top to hold the float," he said easily as he showed her each step. He picked up an empty coffee can from the table and set it on a little round shelf of the separator. "Cream comes out of the top spout and goes into this can and the skim milk comes out of the bottom spout and into the slop bucket for the pigs." He put a filter into a strainer and set that on the big bowl of the separator. Next he poured in milk from the bucket, turned the handle of the separator until it was going at the speed he wanted, and then turned the spigot to let milk flow into the separator. When he finished, he explained that sometimes they kept enough whole milk for the kitchen and let the calf have the rest. "To wash all the parts, we just take the whole thing apart like I put it together."

"Gee, I hope I'll remember all that and be able to do it right," Kate said.

He pointed to the double cement tubs. "We wash the separator in one of these and rinse it in the other with hot water from the teakettle. Now let's go eat."

One of the big pancakes, a small piece of bacon, and an egg was almost more than Kate could handle, but she made a valiant effort to finish it all. Charlie chatted in his usual manner about the day ahead of them. Jake said nothing more than to ask Kate to pass the bacon. Kate was quick to go for the coffeepot to refill the men's cups. She was glad when both men got up from the table, gathered their own place settings, and carried them into the kitchen. She breathed a sigh of relief when she heard the outer door close. When the table was cleared and water was heating for the washing up, Kate wandered to the Dutch door and watched the two men hitch the team just as they had the day before. Under different circumstances she would have enjoyed watching this everyday chore of ranch life. But for now, nothing could soothe her anxiety about the months ahead.

CHAPTER SEVEN

Kate carefully disassembled the separator in reverse of what she had watched Charlie do earlier that morning. She took the disks off the shaft and held them in one hand while she slipped the rod back through holes of the disks in perfect order. She put all the parts into the big supply bowl and carried it to the tub, then did just what she remembered her grandmother doing each morning. She rinsed each part with cold water. Using hot water and soap first would make the dishcloth slimy, her grandmother had told her. She brought hot water from the reservoir on the stove and washed each piece carefully. When all the parts were washed, rinsed with scalding water, and in a drainer, she hung the rack back on the nail. She washed the strainer and milk bucket. "So there, Mr. McClary!" she said aloud when she decided everything was where it should be.

Kate swept the kitchen and mudroom and heated water to scrub the floor. Before the morning was over she had begun a rather thorough cleaning of the kitchen. She ended her chores just before eleven. *These men may know how to cook, but they've got something to learn about keeping a house clean.* Kate was proud of how much she had accomplished and it made her feel good to do manual work again.

With sunshine streaming through the windows and no wind disturbing the snow, Kate decided to put on her down coat and mittens along with her snow boots and explore the place. Everything was covered with snow except where the rock face of the bluff off to the left at the end of the lane came right down to what must be the same creek, bordered with willows, that ran through the Orland Ranch. She went the length of the porch to the west and could see snow-covered meadows for a long ways along the foothills of the mountains to the northwest.

She walked out the mudroom door on the east side of the house and down to the corrals and barn buildings. She assumed that the big metal building across a wide-open space from the barn was for storing machinery. A big red barn sat in the corral that led into two other corrals. She hoped someday to explore the cabin just past the barn that Charlie said had been the original homestead.

Mangers held hay where a milk cow and three horses were munching. Two young pigs came running up as Kate passed the pigsty. She laughed, thinking they were expecting something to eat. She paused where chickens were scratching in the chicken-wire enclosure around the front of a small log building that had a tiny door for the chickens to go in and out. Coming back toward the house she noticed an oval-shaped water trough at the edge of the corral right next to the hill, and water was running into it through a pipe from inside the hill. She guessed that it might come from the overflow of the cistern Charlie told her was buried up there. A pipe at the bottom of the trough carried the excess water down to a creek to the north of the barns and corrals. So far, the water hadn't frozen.

Kate trudged through the snow down the road to get a better view of the front of the house. *Of course, I should have seen it when Charlie and I were coming back from that attempt to drive out of here, but I was too upset.* She stopped where she could see the house in its setting. *A perfectly beautiful log house. And so right for this mountain valley.* She silently approved of the pole fence around the yard and admired the two pine trees and another two cottonwood trees. None of the trees obstructed the view from the living room and kitchen windows.

Kate stood a moment to look out over the meadow to the east. There were hills that curved around and, though unseen, her grandparents' ranch buildings nestled in that end of the valley. The green pine trees looked dark blue up along the edge of the forest line. It was picture-perfect.

Before she started dinner, she put the separator together; she even fastened the filter in the strainer and set it in the big bowl. The potatoes were mashed, the steak fried, and she was making cream gravy when she heard Charlie and Jake come through the outer door a few minutes before two o'clock.

"Smells good," Jake said in a kind tone that surprised her.

Charlie came in right behind Jake and added that it sure was good to have a meal ready for them. "It's cold out there and I'm hungry as a bear."

Kate smiled at him. At least she would have a good friend in Charlie. *It's too bad Jake is so surly most of the time. It wouldn't kill him to crack a smile once in a while.*

They ate the meal mostly in silence, each lost in their own world. After they finished, Kate began to clear the table. "I didn't have time to make anything for dessert," Kate apologized.

Jake gave her a derisive look. "Well, what have you been doing all day?"

"The kitchen needed cleaning," she said defensively, as she passed him canned pears and store-bought cookies. While the two men ate the pears and cookies, Kate brought the coffeepot in to refill their cups.

Charlie looked up and smiled. "Good coffee, Kate," he said, and held his cup for her to fill.

"Where did you learn to make cowboy coffee?" Jake asked.

"From you, this morning," she replied.

Jake acknowledged her comment with a tilted nod of his head. She was glad she had been paying attention that morning when Jake poured cold water in the boiling coffee before moving the pot aside to a cooler area of the stove.

After the meal, both men sat drinking their coffee. Kate overheard them talking about a horse and the weather. She remembered how the men on her grandpa's ranch always talked about ranch work or the weather if they had time to relax after eating. "Are you through with your cups?" she asked, wanting to finish up the dishes before she sat down to read. They both nodded.

"Since we eat dinner so late in the day, we only need cereal or leftovers for supper," Jake said as he scooted his chair back and got up.

Always bossy, she thought, irritated at his manner.

Jake went down the steps into the living room and put a couple of logs in the fireplace. At the same time, Charlie put more kindling in the kitchen stove.

"Just as well take it easy the rest of the afternoon," Charlie said. "We usually read or take a nap."

Kate dried her hands and debated with herself whether to go into the bedroom to read or sit in front of the fireplace. The fireplace won out. It was much warmer there. Jake had stretched out on the couch along the wall. Kate settled into a recliner in front of the fire, next to where Charlie was sitting. He was already nodding off.

In spite of her restless night, Kate didn't nap. The room felt cozy, especially with the afternoon sun filtering in on the west side. Her thoughts kept wandering to David and Jeremy as she tried to concentrate on reading the mystery book she had found on the bookshelf. She looked up when Jake leaped off the couch and nudged Charlie.

"Come on, Charlie, it's time to visit Mrs. Cowley."

"Mrs. Cowley? Who's that?" Kate asked.

Charlie laughed. "She's an old roan-colored mama cow who has beautiful babies—and she provides us with milk."

"I suppose the cat and dog have funny names too?"

"Nope," Jake said. "The dog is Buster and the cat is Jerry. We should have named that cat Lazy for no more than he does around here."

The men each ate a big helping of cornflakes for supper. Kate had a small bowl of the same. Jake and Charlie didn't drink coffee at suppertime so water from the pump was icy cold and seemed to suit both of them just fine. Charlie said they didn't wash the separator at night but the milk bucket and strainer still had to be washed.

Passing the time before she could wash the milk bucket, Kate sat on a stool at the counter looking at a cookbook by the light of the lamp. Jake came in from milking and started the separator.

"Oh, hell," Jake yelled from the milk room.

Kate was horrified when she opened the door and saw milk running all over the floor.

"Apparently you didn't pay attention. The cream spout goes on the top!" Jake said angrily, trying to get the separator to shut down.

"I'm sorry," Kate replied.

"There's rags under the sink. Bring me one—a big one." Jake had switched the spouts and had begun turning the handle again by the time she returned with a wet rag.

She went down on one knee to wipe the floor.

"Leave it, I'll do it." Jake said.

"No, you won't," she said defiantly. When the floor was clean and she had rinsed the rag and hung it to dry, she waited until Jake finished separating then hurried to wash the milk bucket and strainer so she could escape to her bedroom.

———•———

On Monday morning, Jake said he'd be going out to the mailbox when they got in that afternoon. He had mail for the mailman to collect the next day. Without looking at Kate, he said curtly, "If you have any letters or anything you want mailed, you can give them to me when Charlie and I come back from feeding."

While the men were out feeding the cattle, Kate wrote letters to Margo and Cameron and Jean Wyatt. She told them that she was snowed in on a ranch after two ranchhands had pulled her car out of a snowdrift and she expected to be stranded for three or four months. She carefully worded how busy she was helping with cooking and cleaning, but also enjoying the peace and quiet. She avoided mentioning that there were just the two men on the ranch and let them assume there was a wife and kids around. Kate had her mail ready to go when Jake and Charlie came in for dinner. After they had eaten, Jake picked up her letters on the counter without a word to her and left for the mailbox. He hadn't spoken to her since morning, didn't speak to her when he came back, and still didn't during their light supper. Kate saw Charlie's tight expression and irritated sigh as he watched Jake take a lamp to the living room to read. Jake was making it plenty clear that he didn't want her there and Kate couldn't take any more of his silent brooding. The more she thought about it, the more she knew what she had to do.

CHAPTER EIGHT

Jake and Charlie brushed snow from their coats and hats before they went into the mudroom. In the kitchen, Charlie lifted the lid of a roaster on top of the stove. "This looks good," he said, raising the stove lid to stoke the fire. "The fire's gone out. Kate must have gone to sleep." He started to rebuild the fire while Jake dipped tepid water from the reservoir and went to wash up.

The fire was going and Charlie had just taken out water for his own wash when Jake came back into the kitchen. "Seems chilly in here. I'd better check the fireplace," he said. In the dining room, the table was already set. At Jake's place, a piece of paper with several bills on top caught his eye. He picked up the note. "Good lord," he bellowed. "What has she done now?" He stood by the table, arms folded, a tight expression on his face when Charlie approached. "Read that," Jake ordered.

With some apprehension, Charlie picked up the note and read aloud:

> *I'm sorry to have intruded here. I've gone out to meet the mailman and I'll leave the skis by the box. I'll come for my car when the snow is gone.*
> *Kate*

"Well, she's done it this time. And in another snowstorm to boot," Jake said, expelling his frustration.

"We've got to go after her."

"Nope, let her go."

Charlie couldn't believe his ears. "She could be lost out there. At least let's be sure she made it to the mailbox," he argued.

Jake turned toward the kitchen.

"Jake, what's the matter with you?" Charlie said sharply.

Jake stopped in his tracks. It wasn't like Charlie to confront him, or anyone for that matter.

"The truth is, I don't blame her for wanting to get away from you. You've been downright nasty to her and she's a sweet young woman who doesn't deserve to be treated like that."

"Well, is she going to threaten to leave every time she gets upset about something? We can't be chasing after . . ."

Charlie interrupted him in mid-sentence. "I'm going to go after her and see if she made it okay."

"No, you won't. I'm gonna go, but if she's out there froze to death I'm not taking the blame for it." He stomped out to the mudroom. Jake knew Charlie didn't have the stamina at his age to ski out to the mailbox and carry a half frozen woman back to the house.

Once Jake was out on the lane, he could see that the drifting snow had nearly covered the tracks of Kate's skis. He began to think the worst possible: maybe the mailman hadn't been able to get there today, Kate had fallen and hurt an ankle, a moose had come out from the willows and trampled her. His worry intensified when he spotted the mailbox in the distance and couldn't see any skis propped against it.

When Jake reached the mailbox, the mailman had left the weekly newspaper, a catalog, and a couple of letters and magazines. There were no ski tracks. Jake put the mail into the bag he was carrying and retraced his tracks to the path that led from the ranch road. *Maybe Kate went straight ahead instead of turning where she should have. Would she have headed for the bluff off to the left?* As far as he could tell, it wouldn't have offered much protection, and the prairie was windblown and stark. It was as if Jake was seeing it for the first time, how barren it all looked. Thinking how short the days had been growing and what little time he had to search, he hurried back to where the road rose out of the lane and searched for ski tracks. Five minutes later, he saw faint traces of the path she'd taken. He'd gone about a mile when he spotted Kate's figure huddled by a rock that afforded little shelter from the cold. He pushed on as fast as he could ski. Finally he slid to a stop in front of her.

Kate looked up. "I know," she said wearily through stiff lips. "I already know what you're going to say." She padded her mittens together.

"Kitty, you seem determined to freeze yourself to death one way or the other."

"I'm sure you don't care if I freeze myself to death."

Jake gave her a look of disbelief that she would say such a thing. "You're damned stubborn, but I'm not leaving you here to deliberately kill yourself. Now get up. We're going back to the house." He reached for her hand. Reluctantly, she took it and struggled to stand up. Jake helped Kate get her frozen boots back into the bindings of her skis. Her hands were numb and she barely managed to grip the ski poles. She followed his tracks and after a while her stiff limbs began to work better and she was able to keep up, even though he was going slow for her sake and swearing about it under his breath. Kate didn't really care what he thought or did.

Back at the house, Charlie had brewed some tea, even tried to drink some but mostly he paced back and forth waiting for them to return. He saw them coming down the lane and opened the door before they reached the porch. He fussed about Kate so much that she wished he would just let her crawl under the covers and hide. Instead, she drank the warm tea he put in front of her and tried to eat some meat and vegetable broth from the roaster. She didn't have much of an appetite, even after all the strenuous exercise she'd gotten.

Finally Kate spoke up. "I'd really like to turn in now."

"I put some hot water bottles in your bed to warm it up," Charlie said.

"Charlie, you would have made a good doctor. I'll recommend you to the hospital in Jackson if I ever get there."

Jake and Charlie were amused and somewhat surprised at Kate's bit of humor as they bid her good night.

Charlie sat quietly until Jake joined him at the table. "I see Kitty was in such a hurry to get away that she didn't wash the separator. I guess I'll milk enough for the pigs and turn the calf in tonight," Jake said, mostly to make conversation. He glanced at Charlie. "You're awful quiet."

"So, she didn't wash the separator. So she mixed up the spouts when you went to separate. What of it? She's not used to how things are done around here. You criticize everything she does, and never have a kind word for her," Charlie said heatedly.

Charlie seldom complained about anything, but right now he was worked up with such intensity that Jake looked at him, dumbfounded.

"Another thing, you insist on calling her Kitty just because you know she doesn't like that name." He put up a hand to stop Jake who was about to say something. "Laurie left you . . . but Laurie didn't die. Kate's husband and baby both died in a car crash a few months ago. Losing your spouse like that is a whole lot worse than losing a person who could come back. It's been three years since Martha died and I will never stop missing her."

Jake had experienced firsthand how Charlie had suffered with Martha's illness and her prolonged death.

"Okay, you're right. When Kate's skis weren't at the mailbox, I realized she might be lying dead out there and it would be my fault. You know I don't want that on my conscience."

"Just give her a chance. She's tried real hard to take care of us. We should be ashamed if we don't do the same for her." Charlie got up, carried his mug to the kitchen, and went out the door to finish up some chores.

———•———

Kate hesitated to acknowledge Jake the next morning, but she relaxed a little when Jake asked her how she was feeling. He didn't mention what had happened the day before, but asked her if she wouldn't mind scrambling some eggs while he flipped the pancakes. Breakfast was on the table as soon as Charlie finished separating the milk.

As the weeks passed, the days became routine. Kate gathered the eggs and locked the chickens in the chicken house in the late afternoons. Sometimes the eggs needed to be cleaned before she used them and neither Jake nor Charlie had been very careful about that. She had learned early on about replenishing the sourdough starter. Since there was yeast in the storeroom, she usually made bread and rolls with yeast, but they liked her sourdough bread as well. She churned the butter and kept plenty of buttermilk because her buttermilk biscuits were one of their favorites. Suspecting that Jake had been raised Catholic, Kate followed the church rule not to serve meat on Friday. Neither of the men seemed to mind. She made a hefty portion of macaroni and cheese or salmon patties or whatever suited and had it ready when they got in from feeding. She had silently said grace and made the sign of the cross before she ate, until one day Jake asked her to offer grace for all of them. He was still cool toward Kate at times but he didn't speak as harshly and once in a while even tried to engage her in conversation.

Kate also made sure they had dessert after every meal. Charlie said she made apple pie that could win a blue ribbon at the state fair. Jake wanted to know how it was that a city girl like her could bake such a good pie. Her reply that her grandmother was a good teacher brought no response from him, but she'd known all along that he hadn't expected her to be so capable of earning her keep. Baking sometimes proved to be a challenge. The wood stove's oven didn't have a temperature gauge like she had relied on at home so Kate had to open the oven door to see how the baking was going. Once, she made a one-layer cake and opened the oven door to check on it when Jerry suddenly ran past her.

It startled her and she let go of the door. Even though she had used a potholder, the knuckles of her hand hit the hot metal. In spite of the cold water she ran over them, blisters raised on three fingers. To add to her distress, the slam of the door had made the cake fall. Kate was near tears by the time Jake and Charlie got home that day.

"What's this?" Jake asked, looking at the pan of sodden cake.

"The cat ran by and startled me and the oven door slipped out of my hand. When it slammed shut, it made the cake fall."

"Well, maybe we could call it pudding," Jake offered.

"Sure, cream on top will fix it right up," Charlie said. Later when she passed the mashed potatoes to Jake, Charlie saw the blisters on her fingers. He insisted on washing and rinsing the dishes so Kate wouldn't have to put her blistered fingers in hot water.

Jake said he would fill the wood box and "do the hard work while you warm your hands in the dishwater, Charlie." He teased when he added, "Charlie sure looks out for you, Kate. I think he's sweet on you."

"Oh, go on," she said, grinning at Charlie. "I'm kinda sweet on him too."

Charlie gave Jake a "so there" stare and hung up the tea towel.

———•———

Since reading at night by a coal oil lamp wasn't very satisfactory, they all went to bed soon after supper. Kate would be awake by the time she heard one of the men stoking up the fires in the morning. Breakfast was routine too. The men liked bacon or ham, fried eggs, pancakes, and coffee. About the only change they cared about was a switch to sausage and sausage gravy on biscuits now and then.

Sometimes, instead of reading or napping, Jake and Charlie spent the afternoon in highly contested games of cribbage. Kate left them to themselves, thankful that nothing was expected of her.

After Charlie had shown her how to operate the gas washing machine and how to rotate the wringers over the rinse tubs, Kate spent Monday mornings washing clothes. It was never warm enough to hang anything outside so she hung the wet clothes on a rack along the wall, as well as on a line stretched from one end of the mudroom to the other.

A few days before Thanksgiving, Kate had cleaned the house from top to bottom, even Jake's room with his permission. His door had always been closed so she was a bit surprised to see how neat he kept his room.

Kate's last task was to wash the smoke and grime from the tall windows in the living room, the ones above the porch roof. She found an old rickety wooden ladder hanging on the inside wall of the garage and managed to get it in through the door. She braced it as well as she could and set to work. When she had only the highest angled windows left to do, she cautiously climbed higher on the ladder so she could reach the top. After she'd gotten them sparkling clean, Kate dropped her wiping rags to the floor and carried the bucket in her right hand as she descended the ladder. She predicted that Charlie might notice the work she had done, but she wasn't sure about Jake. His general reticence usually kept him from giving a well-deserved compliment anyway.

"What the hell are you doing on that rickety ladder?" Jake yelled, startling her.

Kate's foot missed the next rung. She fell sideways, throwing the bucket of water into the room and twisting her ankle as she landed in the dirty water. The ladder bounced off one of the chairs and crashed down on her left side. She lay gasping with pain that shot through her left shoulder and right leg.

Jake tried to help her up. "I was doing just fine until you yelled at me." He put one hand under her shoulder and the other on her arm. "Leave me alone," she said trying to pull away.

"Quit being so stubborn and let me help you," Jake said, and then promptly picked her up. She hurt too much to protest as he carried her to her bed and carefully laid her down. She fell back on the pillow, her ankle throbbing.

"I'm sorry, Kate. But you shouldn't have used that old ladder," he said sternly. "Where are you hurt?" he asked.

"My ankle mostly."

Jake gingerly took off her shoe and woolen sock before he pulled the extra pillow under her swelling ankle. "We've got to get some ice on that."

Charlie came to the door of Kate's bedroom. "What happened?" he asked.

"I fell off the ladder," Kate said, trying to get up from the bed.

He walked over to Kate and took her hand in his. "Go get some ice or something," he said to Jake.

"That's where I was headed." Jake stepped back reluctantly, not sure he was ready to let Charlie take over.

"Go on, before her ankle starts to swell," Charlie said.

"We have to get that mess cleaned up," Kate said.

Charlie gently pushed her back onto the pillow. "Never you mind . . . we'll take care of that."

Jake returned with some snow in a plastic bread sack that he had wrapped in a towel. Both of them tried to make Kate as comfortable as they could. Charlie fluffed her pillows while Jake brought over another blanket.

Kate assured them she would be okay. "Go eat the stew I left on the stove. You'll have to cut some bread for yourselves." She tried to readjust herself in the bed and winced in pain.

It wasn't long before Charlie was back with a bowl of stew and a slice of Kate's homemade bread. He insisted that she eat what she could and assured her that the mess was cleaned up and the old ladder was back where it belonged.

Jake came in with a pair of crutches. "I found these in the storeroom. Mom used them once when she had a sprained ankle and they came in handy when ol' Clancy bucked me off one time. Anything else I can do?"

"No, Charlie will help me," Kate said, dismissing his offer abruptly.

Charlie helped her manage the crutches enough so she could get to the bathroom. When she came back, she was exhausted and her head ached. She asked Charlie to look in the black bag near the dresser to find her some aspirin.

He opened the bag and found a blood pressure cuff, medicines, and a lot of other medical supplies. "Does a nurse carry around all this medical stuff?"

"No, my husband was a doctor. This was his bag. He and two other doctors were volunteers in a village in South America. They went there together every six months or so. He died just a few days before he was supposed to leave. There's pain medication in there but the aspirin will do."

Charlie brought her a glass of water and Kate took the aspirin. "Is there anything you need?" he asked.

"No thanks, Charlie. You've taken good care of me. You'd better help Jake with the chores."

"I'll let you rest, but holler if you need something. I'll check on you later. Be sure this door is open so you won't get too cold and we can hear you if you call."

After Charlie left, Kate was surprised to see Buster in the doorway. It hadn't taken long for the dog to become enamored with Kate, especially since she saw to his feeding and made sure he had water. Every day Buster accompanied Jake and Charlie to the fields, but he went immediately to Kate as soon as he came into the house. Now, it seemed as if he knew something was wrong.

"Come here, Buster," she urged. The dog moved to the bed and nuzzled her as she ran her fingers through his short dense hair, then he settled down on the rug next to her bed.

In spite of the nagging pain, Kate fell asleep and was quite surprised in the morning to realize she had slept most of the night.

 ## Chapter Nine

Kate quickly got used to the crutches but thought they were an awful nuisance. Her ankle still hurt some but she was eager to put on a traditional Thanksgiving dinner for the three of them. On Wednesday morning she ventured out to the log building that served as a meat house. It was as cold as a freezer and had kept a couple of small turkeys as frozen as when they first came from the grocery store. She brought one into the house so it would have time to thaw. The storeroom supplied all the fixings she needed for what she hoped would be a special meal. Why she was anxious to make it special, she wasn't quite sure. Maybe because both of the men seemed to enjoy the meals she cooked for them. At least Charlie was genuinely appreciative and said so time and again. Jake's compliments were seldom more than, "I'll have another piece of that pie," or "This roast sure cooked up tender." Since falling off the ladder, Kate tried not to think too much about what Jake thought of her or her cooking, but when she sensed more tolerance than pleasure in his attitude, she didn't feel much appreciated.

On Thanksgiving Day, Jake and Charlie went out to feed as usual. They assured Kate they had hauled in extra loads for the mangers the day before so they should be in around one o'clock. She was dishing up potatoes and gravy along with green beans and hot rolls to serve with roast turkey by the time they came in the door.

"Sure smells good in here," Jake said. "But you shouldn't be on that ankle so much."

"I'm fine, it was only a sprain."

Jake looked at Kate skeptically.

"Really, it doesn't hurt much anymore and it is Thanksgiving, you know. You had obviously counted on having a real Thanksgiving dinner because everything was here for one. I didn't find any marshmallows for the sweet potatoes, though," she joked while pouring the rich brown gravy into a pottery bowl.

Both men enjoyed the meal so much that their compliments almost embarrassed Kate.

"My mother is a good cook but you've got her beat with your rolls," Jake said. She found his praise heartwarming and she decided he really did like her cooking. Then when she brought out the pumpkin pie, he smacked his lips and said, "That looks delicious, but let's leave it for supper, I'm stuffed."

"Me too," Charlie chimed in. "Couldn't eat another bite."

The men insisted on doing the dishes while Kate put away the food. Afterward, all three of them fell asleep, with Jake stretched out on the sofa and Charlie and Kate relaxing in the recliner chairs in front of the fireplace. She hardly had time to prop a pillow under her ankle before Jerry jumped into her lap. Later, neither she nor the cat stirred when the men left to do chores. It wasn't until she heard Jake and Charlie come into the kitchen that Kate rubbed her eyes and woke up from a sound sleep.

Hot tea and pumpkin pie with whipped cream drew further enthusiastic oohs and ahs from Charlie and Jake.

It pleased her when Charlie asked, "Where did you learn to make pumpkin pie like that?"

"From her grandmother, of course," Jake said with a wink to Kate.

Kate went to bed that night feeling good about Thanksgiving Day. She was glad that both Jake and Charlie seemed comfortable teasing her about her grandmother and all she'd learned from her after she regaled them with stories of this and that. What's more, she and Jake had acted civil toward each other for the first time since her fall from the ladder. By the next week her ankle seemed to be okay again.

Two days of snowstorms left the pristine meadows glistening, inviting Kate to cross-country ski. Her ankle had healed quite well and she no longer needed crutches. She found a pair of ski boots that fit fairly well and she pulled her socks up over her ski pants. The snow was perfect for skiing. She had been a downhill skier, so cross-country skiing was different but invigorating and the deep snow had crusted enough to hold her up. She soon fell into the rhythm of keeping the poles moving in time with pushing off with one foot and then the other. The scenery was breathtaking and made her feel like a small part of the wide-open space of the meadows before her. The mountains to the north and east seemed majestic even with heavy snow bowing the branches of pine and aspen. Willows along the creek were bearing the weight of their winter coat too. After a half hour, her ankle protested the strain and she headed for the house.

Back at the Bunkhouse she stoked the fires and curled up in front of the fireplace with a cup of hot tea. As was his custom, Jerry jumped on her lap for some attention. From this day on Kate often went out skiing in the mornings, exploring up and down the creek and out into the fields along the mountainsides. Occasionally she saw a coyote or two hovering at the edge of the meadow and one time she saw a moose down by the willows. When she mentioned that she had seen a moose, both Charlie and Jake were alarmed.

"You have to be careful about getting too close to a moose. We don't have many up here but even one can be dangerous," Jake said.

"I guess I wasn't thinking about a moose being in those willows. He wasn't real close, anyway."

After that warning, Kate steered clear of the creek where willows provided plenty of hiding spots for moose. Jake suggested that she ski out to where they were feeding the cattle and she could hang onto a rope attached to the hay sled and glide along behind.

She tried it but it was too hard to stay in the frozen tracks of the horses and sled or in the space between them so she preferred to ski alongside the hay sled. Sometimes she skied on ahead if she wanted to prepare something for their dinner while they finished unloading hay in one of the corrals. She always managed to have their dinner ready by the time they finished feeding. Usually, one or the other would wash or dry the dishes for her.

One day, she had finished in the kitchen and was passing through the dining room to sit before the fireplace to read. Jake caught her arm as she walked by his chair. "Kate, sit down right here. We're going to show you how to play cribbage."

"Okay," she said, putting aside her book. By the time they had instructed her with all the fifteen twos, fifteen fours, and all the other counting, and how to move the pegs in the cribbage board, Kate was fascinated with the game.

"Okay now, you beat Charlie on your own. I'm going to feed the fires," Jake said. When he returned a short time later, he pointed out which cards she should hold and even counted the points before she could figure them out for herself. Jake challenged her to a game and fussed at Charlie for giving her too much help. Kate laughed when he chided Charlie for doing the very same thing he had done, but she was beginning to understand the game pretty well. They traded off games with her until it was time to do the chores. From then on, cribbage became a regular afternoon pastime, unless both of the men begged off to read or take a nap.

It was becoming more and more apparent to Kate that the men had strenuous work harnessing horses—they were using four horses on the sled now—then feeding all the animals and doing the milking twice a day. They never seemed to be bored or restless, but they did come in cold and tired every day. Of course, the days were short and there was a lot to do during every day but nights were long so they rested then. She knew from all her grandparents had told her that each season had its own work to be done.

———•———

On a Tuesday, in the first week of December, two letters came for Kate. They were postmarked several days apart. It was growing dark by the time Jake came in with the mail and Kate didn't want to wait until morning to read the letters, so she placed a lamp on the table next to the sofa and opened the earlier postmarked one. It was from Margo. Jerry moved onto her lap as was customary and Kate caressed his silky fur as she savored the news from her friends. Both Margo and the Wyatts had been surprised to hear what had happened to her. They expressed concern about her and asked that she keep them informed as best she could. *They'd probably send out a posse if they knew the whole truth—that I'm here alone with two men. But what am I thinking? Even a posse couldn't get through all this snow.*

She read Margo's letter again. Margo hurried through the formalities before launching into a detailed account of a new romantic interest in her life. She had been going with Steve for several weeks and he was the most wonderful man she had ever met. Kate smiled when she read this. She had heard Margo say the same thing twice before and the next thing she knew they had broken up. *Maybe Margo has met the right man this time.* As she read on, Kate realized how serious it sounded.

The next day, Kate answered the letters and left them on a counter in the kitchen. Jake skied out Sunday afternoon so they would be there for the mailman on Tuesday. Kate had offered several times to take the mail out or to collect it, but Jake said she didn't know the way well enough and besides it was a four-mile round trip. He said it would be too much for her. Privately, Kate was relieved that he refused her help because she did have some apprehension about doing it on her own. Nonetheless, she was glad she made the offer.

Receiving letters and getting the local weekly newspaper as well as a couple of magazines was a high point in her week. Even though she craved to read more state and national news, Kate realized that the mailman couldn't possibly carry a load of daily papers every week, so she simply looked forward to anything that came. She had written several Christmas letters that she hoped would arrive at their destination in time for her friends to have an address for her.

On a quiet afternoon in mid-December Kate asked Jake and Charlie if they'd like to play a game she brought with her. They eyed her skeptically as she headed to her room and returned with a Scrabble set. Both men said they had played a few times and were willing to give it a go. Charlie, who wasn't the best speller of the three and who tried to spell a word the way it sounded even if it wasn't the proper spelling, was a great sport. She and Jake, though, were especially competitive and often called the other on the use of a questionable word.

One afternoon as they were putting away the tiles after a stimulating game that Kate had decidedly won, Charlie spoke up, "Living in the Bunkhouse isn't as bad as you thought it would be, is it, Kate?"

"No, I enjoy the peace and quiet. Although this was not exactly a quiet afternoon," she laughed.

"Well, we had to put up a fight on those two uncommon words you used. Otherwise, you'd think we were really lame," Jake said.

"But we had to concede when you showed them to us in the dictionary," Charlie added. "And you were really clever when you added the word "house" to Jake's "bunk."

Kate frowned. "Which reminds me, why do you call this house the Bunkhouse? I thought the bunkhouse was where the hired men lived on a ranch."

"That's right," Jake said, running a hand through his thick curly hair. "Soon after we finished the house, your grandma and grandpa came to see it, and ol' George told Dad, 'This is a pretty fancy bunkhouse you've built here, Will.' So we've called it the Bunkhouse ever since."

"That's wonderful!" Kate already liked the house but now it had a special meaning for her knowing that her grandfather had named it.

In spite of the camaraderie that was growing amongst the three of them, Kate still had moments of deep grief and a sense of guilt about finding some peace in the aftermath of losing David and Jeremy. She supposed that it was these uneasy feelings that kept her nightmares occurring. She hadn't shared much about this with Jake and Charlie, but kept it to herself, hopeful that her upsetting dreams would disappear gradually. Sundays were the hardest for her. She had seldom missed Sunday Mass. Reading the Bible or praying the rosary didn't take the place of receiving the sacrament of Communion. Nevertheless, she read from her missal and Bible on Sunday mornings and usually prayed her rosary before she went to sleep that night. And now she was painfully aware that Christmas was approaching. The sadness she felt about her son not experiencing the childhood joy and excitement of Christmas time wrapped around her like a dark cloud. Each day, while Jake and Charlie were out taking care of the cattle, she asked God to give her the strength to see her through this holiest of seasons.

Charlie sensed how difficult this time of year must be for Kate. He spoke with Jake about it as they were heading back to the Bunkhouse one day. Jake said there wasn't much they could do about it and suggested they let her be. Charlie insisted they do something to cheer her up but for the time being his pleas fell on deaf ears.

Then about a week later Jake stomped into the kitchen with an unusually mischievous look on his face. "Sorry we're late for dinner," he told Kate.

Charlie was right behind him. "Thought you wouldn't mind since we have a surprise for you."

"Really, what is it?" Kate asked.

"Come see," Charlie said, leading her into the dining room. Jake opened the door and swept his arms wide in a deep bow to Kate.

Propped up on the porch was a beautiful pine tree. Kate drew in a quick breath. Her first thought was of Jeremy and how excited he would have been to see such a big tree. She glanced from Charlie to Jake. Both of them had wide grins on their faces, indicating how proud they were of themselves.

"This is a wonderful surprise. You know, in the city we had to buy a tree. Shall I make popcorn and paper cut-outs to decorate it?"

"No, we aren't that old fashioned," Jake said. "We do have some decorations around somewhere."

"Okay, let's find them after dinner," Kate said with all the enthusiasm she could gather.

Jake sobered. "Christmas must be a hard time for you this year after losing your family. We weren't too sure if you'd even want a tree."

She turned from the tree and spoke directly to both of them. "You're right. I wanted to see Jeremy's excitement on Christmas morning and enjoy a quiet Christmas with David, as we always did." She pressed her hand to her mouth for a long moment then looked up again. "But this tree is like a symbol—that life goes on and we must go on too. I love the tree. It's a great surprise."

After dinner, Jake offered to set up the tree while Kate and Charlie looked for decorations in a couple of boxes in the storeroom. By chore time, the six-foot tree was decorated with ornaments and tinsel. Kate asked Jake not to throw away the branches he had trimmed from the bottom of the tree so she could make a wreath out of them.

Later they sat in the living room and watched how the ornaments reflected the light from the fireplace, which made the tinsel shimmer even brighter.

No one had much to say. Eventually Kate took a deep breath and said, "This tree gives off such a wonderful pine aroma, probably because it's freshly cut, don't you think so?"

The only response was from Jake. "Uh-huh. Nice, isn't it?"

Kate was enchanted with the utter simplicity of the night, with the tree standing before them that came from a hillside on the ranch, and with a sense of peace from being in the wilderness. Not one of them was inclined to disturb the quiet with much conversation. It consoled Kate to realize how calming it all was.

As was his custom, Jake woke an hour or so after midnight and got up to keep the fires burning. He put a split log into the fireplace and had just replaced the screen when a scream pierced the still night. Jake hurried across the room and up the steps to Kate's room.

"No, oh no God, no . . ." Her arms flailed as Jake tried to pull her close.

"Easy, Kate," he murmured against her hair. "You're safe, easy now." He rocked her back and forth, whispering gently until her whimpering and sobs began to subside.

Kate grew still and pulled back enough to look up at him in the dim moonlight. "Jake?"

"It's me. You must have had a bad dream."

She pulled out of his arms but she didn't say anything.

Jake held her shoulders and could feel how badly she trembled. "Kate, let's go in by the fireplace where it's warmer and I'll make some cocoa." He grabbed her chenille robe from the end of the bed. "Here, put this on."

Bewildered, Kate let him help her pull on the robe. "This was the worst one ever."

Covered with a woolen blanket and curled up in the recliner, she sat staring into the flames of the burning logs. The intensity of her nightmare had disoriented her. Jake handed her a mug of hot chocolate.

She snapped back to where she was and what was happening. "I'm sorry I woke you."

"You didn't. I had just put some logs on the fire when I heard you scream. You sure sounded scared."

They sat in silence watching flames dance up and around the

burning logs, aware of the aroma of burning wood mixed with the tang of pine in the room.

"Would you like to talk about it?" Jake asked quietly.

"It's a sad story."

"That's okay."

Kate fastened her gaze on the picture above the mantel of two men on top of a load of hay on a sled pulled by a team of horses, fairly reminiscent of what she had been witnessing for the past few weeks at Jake's ranch. "When I learned that I was snowed in here, I was terribly worried, knowing how much you hated having me here."

Kate raised her hand when she saw that Jake was about to protest.

"I didn't blame you, and you've been kind, really." She pulled the blanket closer. "I met David when I was in nurses' training and he was in medical school. We married soon after he became a doctor. David's father asked David to join his practice in Kansas City. Dr. Webster was a fine man and very much respected in his profession. However, Mrs. Webster disliked me intensely and she never forgave her son for not marrying a girl she had chosen for him . . . a girl of their social class."

"Boy, that's pretty tough. Surely, she liked you once she got to know you."

"No, she never liked me even then, but that doesn't matter anymore." She went on, "David and I really wanted children but we had been married five years before I finally became pregnant. Of course we were happy to have a baby boy. Jeremy was just four months old when he and David were killed."

"I'm so sorry, Kate."

She drew in a long breath and sat quietly for a minute. "David called from the hospital and asked if I would work the evening shift in the emergency room because one of the nurses was sick. I hadn't worked since before Jeremy was born, but I loved being a nurse and usually worked in the emergency room. When David said he would take care of Jeremy, that it would give them a chance to visit his mother, I agreed."

Kate swallowed a sob. "When David and Jeremy were on the way to pick me up a drunk driver ran into them. The ambulance brought them into the emergency room where I was working. They both died there."

"Is that what your nightmare was about?"

"The nightmares are always about seeing David and Jeremy dead in that emergency room. I had hoped the nightmares would go away with time but with Christmas coming up, I'm constantly thinking about never knowing my baby's first Christmas, first birthday, first steps, first words . . ."

They sat in silence for a long time, Kate staring into the fire and Jake with his elbow on the arm of his chair, rubbing his fingertips lightly across his forehead.

"I was pretty nasty to you when you came here," Jake finally said, without looking at Kate. "I wasn't good company for anyone. Charlie will attest to that. Two months before you got here I was supposed to be married and shortly before the wedding, my brother Jesse and I decided to trade ranches." Jake began to feel uncomfortable talking about his own misfortune. "Maybe you'd rather not listen to this tonight. We've got lots of time before the snow thaws and you're probably not caring about my problems right now."

Kate was tired but she wanted to hear Jake out. "No, it's okay. Go on."

"I lived on our grandparents' ranch near Saratoga and Jesse and his family lived here. His wife had been teaching their three kids here at home. The oldest one was about to start junior high. It didn't make sense for Mary Anne and the kids to move to town for school during the winter. If they moved to the Saratoga ranch, all of the kids could go to school and Jesse would be with them. Besides, I had always wanted to live here. They were really excited when I offered to exchange with them."

"That sounds like it should have been a good arrangement," Kate said.

"Charlie and Martha worked for our grandparents on the ranch at Saratoga for a long time. It was awfully hard on him when she died of cancer a few years ago. I was sure glad when he said he wanted to come up here with me."

Kate rotated the mug in her hand and took a sip of the hot chocolate.

"So I brought Laurie to see this place but she was adamant that she wanted to stay where she was. I was sure she would come around."

Kate looked at Jake intently. "First mistake?"

With a wry grin he said, "You know, 'whither thou goest' and all that. But it wasn't like that at all. Jesse and I were about to walk from the sacristy out to the altar when someone handed me a note from Laurie that said if I didn't change my mind about going to 'that god-forsaken place,' she wasn't going to come down the aisle. I'm not too proud of leaving that church full of people sitting there but that ultimatum was enough to make me do it."

"Well, I think she could have given you a little more advance notice," Kate said, sympathetically.

He shrugged his shoulders. "So you see, I wasn't happy about seeing you intruding on my mad pout."

He didn't say anymore but she knew deep down that he wouldn't have been so upset if it had been any other woman intruding on his mad pout. Kate thought about making some peace about the hostility they'd had toward each other in the past, but Jake got up to put another log in the fireplace.

"Think you can sleep now?" he asked.

"I hope so. Thanks for listening to me and telling me about Laurie."

"My experience doesn't hold a candle to what you've gone through. No wonder you have such nightmares."

Kate got up, still wrapped in the blanket and took a few steps toward the stairs.

"I really am sorry about your husband and your baby," Jake said kindly.

She smiled. "It's too bad your marriage didn't work out." She paused as she walked past the Christmas tree. "Would you and Charlie have brought in this beautiful tree if I hadn't been here?"

He shook his head. "Not likely," was all he said.

 **Chapter Ten**

Kate spent several days before Christmas making fudge, divinity, and caramels. She even popped some popcorn, which she and Jake had done a couple of times, but this time she made it into popcorn balls. She had managed to have the sweets done up and hidden before the men came in from feeding.

That evening, Kate was bowled over when Jake asked, "How about some of that popcorn you popped today?"

Her eyebrows lifted quizzically.

"We smelled popcorn when we came in, you know," he laughed.

"Oh, okay. You ruined my surprise, you know," she mocked. She went to the pantry and brought back three popcorn balls.

"Popcorn balls?" Jake chuckled.

"Thought you kids needed a popcorn ball for Christmas," Kate teased.

"This is a real treat," Charlie said, after he'd taken a first bite. "No one ever thought I was kid enough to enjoy something like this."

Kate suspected that Charlie would have said this to please her even if he disliked popcorn balls.

———•———

The following Tuesday Jake skied out as usual to pick up the mail. Kate received several Christmas cards in response to the ones she had mailed out a couple of weeks before. There was a package from Margo, which she put under the tree. She read each of her cards at least twice. Everyone except Margo, Cameron, and Jean, who knew where she was, expressed their surprise and worry about her being snowed in. Most of her friends wrote that they thought of her often and were glad to hear that she was finding some comfort in being out on a ranch, then wished her a Merry Christmas and a better New Year. It pleased Kate to read a letter from Cindy, a nurse Kate liked, who wrote that a memorial plaque had been placed in the hospital lobby honoring both David and his father.

Christmas Eve was just like any other time, there were chores to do, the livestock had to be fed, and there was time for a rest before tackling chores again. While the men were out in the morning, Kate cooked a ham, prepared scalloped potatoes, a Jell-O salad, and a pie.

She finished with the cooking about noon so she decided to have a cup of tea and enjoy the Christmas tree. After putting a log in the fire she spotted a small wrapped package under the tree near Margo's gift. She knelt down and picked it up. "To sweet Katie, from Charlie," the tag read. Tears came to her eyes. She went to her car to do something she had considered doing for several days. She opened the trunk, pulled out a box, and took it into the house. She set it on the dining room table and went to the storeroom where she had seen Christmas wrap in a box with some of the tree decorations. Before she could change her mind or even fret about it, she opened the box, took out the smaller sweater, and wrapped it. Hesitantly, Kate picked up the larger matching sweater. She sat down at the table and caressed the soft wool with a pensive sadness, not quite sure she was able to let go of this part of her past. Grandma Orland had taught her basic knitting patterns and stitches, but for these sweaters she had studied and chosen an Aran pattern with a ninety percent fine lamb's wool and ten percent silk yarn in a moss color. She liked the combination of cable and zigzag stitches. While she ran her fingers over the fabric and remembered how much of herself she had put into making these sweaters, she reaffirmed to herself that no matter what she did with them she had made them with love for David and herself. She folded the sweater and carefully wrapped it too. She had planned to give David his sweater on his birthday. Now that David would never get to wear it, and she would always feel his loss if she wore hers, Kate made up her mind.

David's large one would fit Jake quite well and hers would fit Charlie. Certain that she'd made the right decision, Kate attached the tags and put the packages toward the back of the tree and went about dusting the piano.

It was after four o'clock when the men came in from feeding. They brought in extra hay to the mangers in the corral for the workhorses and milk cow, and then milked, fed the pigs, and gathered the eggs for Kate before they came in. Charlie set the basket of eggs on the counter and took a close look at the pie cooling on a rack nearby.

"This pie looks pretty good and I think it's different than any we've had, huh?"

Kate didn't answer, but gave him a playful mind-your-own-business look. She had on a silky ivory shirtwaist top with its collar turned up, a black woolen ankle-length skirt, and a pair of dressy shoes with little straps over the arch of her feet. She had fastened her hair on the crown of her head with a clip so that it all fell in a silken mass.

"Hmm, another surprise?" Charlie guessed.

"That's right," Kate said matter-of-factly and went right on dishing up their supper. She nearly dropped the big spoon when she heard a wolf whistle.

"You *are* a sight for two old guys' sore eyes," Jake said, looking her up and down.

Kate turned around, felt an unexpected thrill at his admiring look, and said, "Thank you, kind sir."

"You're much too beautiful to be holed up here with a couple of old codgers like us . . . but it's damn nice for us, huh?" Jake concluded, clapping Charlie on the shoulder.

Kate's face warmed with a blush. It almost embarrassed her to hear Jake talk like that, but at the same time she couldn't help being pleased.

"You sure look pretty, Katie. Don't let Jake fool you. I'm the only old codger around here," Charlie said.

They were eating supper when Kate paused between bites to look earnestly at the two men. "Do you two ever take a vacation? You know, go somewhere just to relax and have fun?"

Jake and Charlie looked at each other. Jake asked, "What's a vacation?" The two men cracked up.

"Seriously, you work so hard all winter. Can't you take time to see some of the world? You don't even see movies here."

"We know, but seriously, Kate, it's hard to get away from a ranch for very long. You probably remember. After the winter, there's calving, branding, moving cows to summer pasture, irrigating, haying, selling cattle, and feeding the ones that are left during the winter." Jake ate a couple of bites before he went on. "I suppose it's a vacation to go to the National Finals Rodeo which I've done a few times but it's only for a few days. Usually make Cheyenne Frontier Days for a couple of days too. Actually, I saw quite a lot of the world when I was in the service."

"How about you, Charlie?" Kate asked.

"Martha and I usually took a few days off after haying to go see our families in Colorado. And we went to Arizona for a couple of weeks in the winter when we could get away." He smiled and said, "Wouldn't be much fun to go now, but I'll go see my brother and sister sometime. How about you?"

"The best trip David and I ever took was to Peru where we worked the whole time taking care of patients. It was fun to see the country. I guess doctors don't take vacations very often either," she said with a shrug. "At least, my doctor didn't."

Jake pushed back from the table.

"I'm full as a tick. Let's leave the pie till later."

"Best idea you've had all night," Charlie said.

"Kate, would you play the piano for us?" Jake asked. "There's a book of Christmas carols in that rack by the piano."

"Yes, let's sing some carols," Charlie agreed.

Everyone pitched in to clear the table. Kate put away the leftovers while Jake and Charlie did up the dishes.

Kate played a few measures of "It Came Upon A Midnight Clear." Unbeknownst to her Jake had left the room. When she heard him begin to tune a guitar behind her, she swiveled around. "Well, for heaven's sake, who'd a thought . . ."

"I'm ready," Jake said with a smile.

Charlie sat nearby on the couch and listened to the fine music and the harmonizing of Kate and Jake. When they started singing "Silent Night," Charlie's bass tones blended well with their soprano and tenor voices. As the last note faded away, they clapped their hands together in praise for themselves and carried on into the night with more songs.

Finally Kate's fingers were begging for a rest. "Let's take a break. That was a workout . . . but so much fun," she said.

Charlie strutted over to the tree, filling his stomach with air and feigning Santa Claus as he picked up Kate's gift. "Merry Christmas. This is for you."

"Oh, Charlie, thank you." She held the package in her hand while she went to the backside of the tree and retrieved the packages for them she had hidden. They prompted her to open hers first. Kate carefully unwrapped the small box and when she uncovered a squash blossom necklace in a black velvet case, she instinctively took Charlie's hand and pulled him down next to her on the couch. "It's beautiful."

"Martha and I went to Arizona for our anniversary a few years ago and she saw this turquoise necklace in a Navajo trading post." He pointed to the turquoise setting. "Each turquoise is set in this silver design that was hand stamped, and they called that a blossom. This piece on the point that looks like a horseshoe has matching turquoise and silver. I could see how much Martha loved this necklace so I bought it for her for our anniversary."

"Oh, Charlie, it's really special. Here, help me put it on."

He unfastened the closure and put the necklace around her neck. "She didn't get to wear it much before she died. We never had any children but if we did, we would have wanted a daughter just like you."

Kate wiped away a tear. She leaned over and hugged Charlie tight and whispered, "I'm honored to wear it."

Charlie and Jake opened their packages at the same time. Neither of them said anything for a few moments, they just stared at the handsome sweaters. Finally, Charlie said, "What a nice color. Oh, Katie, I bet you made these, didn't you?"

"Yes, I hoped you would like them."

"You didn't make this for me," Jake said quietly.

"I didn't know you then, but I want you both to have them. I just hope they fit."

Charlie was running his hand over the fine wool when Jake got up and left the room. "Wonder what he's up to."

Kate admired her present. "I've always wanted a turquoise necklace, especially a squash blossom one."

"And the sweater. I don't know where I'll go so I can wear it but I'll find someplace to show it off," Charlie said.

"I made them for my husband and me, but he died before I could give him his. I don't think I could ever wear mine now that he's gone. I hope you don't mind?" she asked tentatively.

"No, I don't mind. Katie, I know this is a tough time for you, especially with Christmas and all."

Kate covered his hand with hers. "I couldn't have asked for a better place or better friends than you and Jake have been to me these past few weeks. It has made it so much easier to accept what has happened and go on with my life."

Jake came from the kitchen and down the steps with his arms full. "These are for you. No more skiing with those old skis, and you need some new boots," he said, trying to sound casual.

Kate looked at the skis, boots, and boxes spilling over with jacket, cap, mittens, and ski pants. "Oh my gosh, I can't accept all that." Quite certain that she was right, she added, "Look, I know you didn't buy those things for me. They were meant for Laurie."

Jake knelt on one knee and looked Kate in the eye. "You're right, of course. I bought them for Laurie but she didn't want them and I'm hoping you do."

She looked at the ski outfit with her thumb and forefinger pulling at her lips. "I don't know . . ." she said uncertainly.

Jake tipped her chin up toward him. "You made this sweater for your husband, right?"

She nodded yes.

"Do you think you can stand to see me wearing it when you made it especially for your husband, the man you loved?"

Kate answered with a steady voice. "Yes."

"Then I'll try it on right now."

Kate hoped the sleeves were long enough but it was such a perfect fit that she relaxed and watched as Jake stroked the soft fabric from elbow to wrist with a pleased look on his face.

Neither Jake nor Kate had seen Charlie slip his sweater over his head. He stood up, spread his arms, and said, "Well, looky here." With a happy grin, he leaned over and said softly, "Thank you very much, Katie. I've never had anything so fine."

She smiled. "You're welcome, Charlie. I'm so glad you like it."

"Oh," Kate said, jumping to her feet, "I almost forgot."

Jake's voice stopped her. "Just a minute, Kate. You've made this a great Christmas for Charlie and me. I want to thank you for this beautiful sweater. I'll enjoy wearing it."

"And I will enjoy skiing in this lovely ski outfit," Kate said, donning the mittens and ski cap he'd given her. She went off to the kitchen thinking how glad she was that she had decided to give Charlie and Jake the sweaters.

When she came back, Jake was using a poker to steady a log on the fire and Charlie had moved to one of the recliners.

"Surprise!" Kate said. She set one of the plates of candy on a side table and handed another to each of the men. They all tried each kind and the men declared she had outdone herself this time. Kate remembered the pie, but none of them thought they could eat another bite.

"What kind did you make?" Charlie asked.

"Another surprise?" Jake chimed in.

"Yes, it's a sour cream raisin pie and the meringue will be all tough by tomorrow."

"Well, maybe we'd better have a little piece?" Jake said, looking at Charlie.

"Oh yes, we don't want that meringue to get tough." They all laughed.

Kate realized her day had been such a busy one that she hadn't given a lot of thought to David and Jeremy until she was lying in bed and praying for them. She was feeling the same guilt about enjoying herself after losing them. She was tired enough that she didn't dwell on what she couldn't change and slept peacefully all night. The week between Christmas and New Year's Eve was like any other week. They played Scrabble every evening, enjoying Charlie's antics when he used five tiles to spell a word. Once Kate used all seven tiles to spell quartzite with the "t" fitting into two other words and the "q" on a triple score square. That added fifty points to an already big score. After that game Jake said they ought to play poker once in a while, but Kate said she didn't know how. He offered to teach her.

"If I learn to play poker, then I think we ought to make bets with money," she said, trying to keep a straight face.

"Better not do that, Jake," Charlie said wryly. "She'd end up owning the ranch."

———— • ————

During the week, Kate dismantled the Christmas tree so they could take it out and set it up in the yard. It was a special Christmas, after all, she decided.

On the morning of New Year's Eve, Jake announced at breakfast that he had a surprise for them to celebrate the New Year.

When Jake and Charlie came in about three that afternoon,

the table was set with china and good silver, which Kate had carefully polished several days ago. She had put on a white linen tablecloth, cloth napkins, goblets, and wine glasses. Kate wore the same outfit as on Christmas Eve, adorned by the turquoise necklace.

Both men went to clean up before they sat down to eat the tender roast beef, mashed potatoes, gravy, green beans, and hot rolls. There were pickles and olives too. She put an extra dish at each plate and poured icy water into the goblets.

"Kate, you made cottage cheese?" Jake said, astonished.

"Grandmother?" Charlie asked.

Kate had a broad smile on her face.

Jake offered to say grace. He said the same words Kate always said, adding, "Thanks Lord, for sending us such a good cook." The three of them crossed themselves.

Did the Lord send me here? I sure never thought of it that way. This crossed Kate's mind as Jake finished grace.

"Well, this *is* special!" Jake said when he tasted the first bite of cottage cheese set in the center of a pear half and topped with a dollop of mayonnaise and a maraschino cherry.

"Katie, I've never had cottage cheese on a pear before but it's downright tasty. And, Jake's right, you sure are a good cook."

The men told Kate they had seen several elk among the aspen trees up on the mountain. "I hope they stay up there. If they start in on a haystack, there's no way to keep them out," Jake said. "One year, we had to put up a slab fence around two haystacks and the fence had to be tall enough that they couldn't jump over it. Jesse said they haven't had much trouble with the elk or moose getting into the stacks the last few years."

"Suppose that's because they didn't have as much snow for a few years?" Charlie asked.

Jake said, "Maybe. There's a lot of snow this year so I sure hope the elk and moose don't bother the hay."

"What about that surprise?" Charlie asked when Jake sat back and patted his full stomach.

"After chores," Jake replied.

 CHAPTER ELEVEN

Later that afternoon, Kate had been dozing off when she heard a commotion in the kitchen. Soon Jake came down the steps into the living room carrying a wet baby calf wrapped in a gunnysack and held it until Charlie laid an old blanket down before the fireplace. Kate knelt before the newborn Jersey calf and wiped him down with an old towel that Charlie had brought along. "You poor thing," she cooed over it, running her fingers through the silky hair and twirling it in the baby's natural curls. He didn't respond much and she began to worry about whether he was going to live. "Isn't it awfully early for a calf to be born?" she asked. "He'd freeze out there."

Jake knelt down on one knee and patted the calf's rump. "Yes, it's way too early. That's why we'll keep him in the house until he's warm. A calf is a big investment for a rancher. Aside from the fact that we are fond of the little buggers, they put the food on our table."

Charlie had been watching Kate stroking the fragile animal. "He's a cute little fellow, isn't he? He's going to come around soon, then he'll be calling for his mama."

Jake caressed the soft hair, curling it around his finger like Kate continued to do. "I bought a milk cow last fall and the guy told me she had been bred . . . he didn't say she was going to calve in January." He took off his Scotch cap.

"In a couple of months Mrs. Cowley will have her own calf," Charlie added. "We'll let her dry up now that we have this little guy's mama to milk."

"Is he hungry? Don't we have to give him a bottle or something?" Kate asked.

Jake spoke. "He sucked for a few minutes until we had to get him dry and warm. We may have to feed him a time or two, but he really needs to get his milk directly from his mama. He's strong, he'll be up and running around before you know it."

"We brought in enough milk to get him through the night," Charlie said.

Jake and Charlie went to wash up. Kate sat beside the newborn, talking softly and stroking his fine hair. She hardly noticed when Jake and Charlie came back into the room, and didn't look up until Charlie cleared his throat. Both men had on new Levi's, fancy cowboy boots, and colorful plaid cowboy shirts with pearl snaps. Jake wore a dark blue neckerchief tied at an angle at his neckline.

"My, my," Kate said. "Is there something going on around here I don't know about?"

"Well, Jake, what about that surprise?" Charlie asked. Jake hadn't told him why he ought to dress up a bit.

"Isn't this baby the surprise?" Kate asked.

"Not entirely, Katie. We knew he was coming," Charlie chuckled.

Jake began moving the chairs to the outer part of the room and pushed aside the round glass-topped wagon wheel coffee table. He walked over to the phonograph and opened the bottom doors. "It's New Year's Eve and we're going to have a dance right here." He pulled out a few records.

"You're kidding," Kate said.

Jake opened the lid and placed a record on the spindle. He turned the handle that wound the phonograph. When the lively music started up, he reached his hand out to Kate. "May I have the first dance?"

Kate put her hand in his and rose to her feet just in time to be swung into a jitterbug. Both easily kept in step with the tempo.

Charlie sat down to watch them. He caught Jake's eye and pointed to Buster crouching by a chair watching their every move. "Look at your bodyguard, Kate. He's wondering if you're safe."

Kate found the dog's eyes fastened on her. "How sweet."

When the music stopped, Jake lifted the needle off the recording. "Your turn, Charlie."

"Make it a waltz, then. 'Blue Danube,' maybe."

They had only made a couple of rounds in the small room when Kate said, "Charlie, you waltz so gracefully. You and Martha must have danced a lot."

"My Martha and I loved to waltz. I haven't danced since I lost her."

Jake watched Kate and Charlie as they twirled around the room, so light on their feet and attuned to each other. When the music ended he lifted the needle and switched off the phonograph. Kate went to the kitchen to slip a peach cobbler into the oven to warm.

When Kate returned, Jake had wound up the phonograph again. "I want to do that waltz with you," he said timidly. "I've only waltzed a few times in my life but it looked easy when you and Charlie were dancing. Hope I don't step on your toes."

She looked him up and down. "I hope not, too," she teased. They stepped easily into the one, two, three rhythm.

"Not bad, huh?" Jake said, grinning down at her. He pulled Kate closer to him.

Jake and Charlie took turns dancing with Kate until she fell in a chair, took a deep breath, and let it out slowly. "Let's rest." Buster walked over and put his head on her lap. "Thanks for looking after me, Buster," she told him, ruffling his thick fur.

"We'd better give that calf some milk. He'll be bawling if we wait much longer," Jake said.

———— • ————

Jake knelt beside the calf with a bucket that had a nipple attached at the lower edge. "Could you hold his head?" he asked Kate. She held the tiny head while he nuzzled around the nipple until he got a mouthful of milk and then went to work on it. When the milk was gone, Jake took the bucket back to the milk room.

Then all three of them headed for the kitchen. Jake carried an oil lamp to the dining table while Charlie carried another to the kitchen. While Kate set the cobbler on the table so they could help themselves and brought in a pitcher of thick cream and a pot of hot tea, Jake collected wine from the cellar. Charlie got three wine glasses from the china cupboard. In the soft glow of the oil lamp, the men had two helpings of the cobbler. Kate ate slowly and sipped the wine.

Kate caught Jake's eye and said, "I haven't danced for so long and tonight I had two great partners."

He shook his head and chuckled. "My mom wouldn't believe I could waltz unless she saw it for herself."

"I wonder what she'd say if she saw you tonight."

"Well, Kate, you're a great partner too. I hope we can do that again one of these days," Charlie said.

"Maybe we ought to have a couple more dances, if Kate would agree," Jake suggested.

"Sure, I'd like that," Kate replied.

It wasn't quite midnight when they all agreed it was time to hit the hay. Kate put her arm through Charlie's, then leaned over and kissed him on the cheek, wishing him a Happy New Year. After that she walked over to Jake who was putting away the records and closing up the phonograph. She stood on her tiptoes and kissed him on the cheek. "Happy New Year," she said.

"Happy New Year, Kate," he whispered and kissed her on her cheek. "It's starting out happy, anyway." He handed her a lamp and she wished them both a good night.

———•———

Sometime during the night, Kate woke up when Jake tossed a log into the fireplace. A moment later, he was talking softly to the baby calf. "It's all gone," she heard him say. Then she drifted back to sleep and came fully awake just before daybreak. The calf was bleating noisily. Kate got up, slipped on her robe and slippers, and by the dim light from the fireplace made her way to the calf.

It was standing up and making quite a racket. Kate wrapped her arms around him and tried to quiet the little bugger.

Before long Jake came into the room, fully dressed and carrying a lantern. "You're spoiling that calf. I'd better take him back out to his mama. I'll get my coat before he makes a mess."

"Too late," Kate told him, dryly.

At dinnertime, Kate told the men she had checked on the calf that morning and he seemed frisky and well fed. "I didn't go in that stall, his mama cow kept a close eye on me when I looked through the gate."

"She's pretty gentle, probably wouldn't hurt you, but it's best to be careful," Charlie agreed.

The next morning, Kate said she was glad the calf and his mama were in the barn. "It's so darn cold out there."

"Only forty-five below this morning," Jake teased.

"I'm glad I can stay in where it's warm," she said, rubbing her arms to bring some warmth to them.

"There should be some long johns in one of those drawers in your room. If you can find them, you're welcome to them. Might even be some wool pants."

Kate didn't waste time after they had gone to feed before she went searching and found the warmer clothes. She warmed them a bit by the stove before taking off her outer clothes and slipping on the long johns. She had seen Jake and Charlie stoking the fires dressed in their one-piece long johns and Levi's and it brought back memories of seeing her grandfather wearing the same type of clothes, even in summertime. Grandma, on the other hand, always wore a cotton dress in the house, often with a warm sweater over it. How Grandma ever stood the harsh cold and hard work on the ranch, not to mention the isolation and loneliness, escaped Kate. But Grandma always accepted life as it happened and never felt sorry for herself, or if she did, she didn't let on to Kate. She never got cabin fever, even though she had known women who became depressed with the long winters and no contact with other people.

To occupy some of the endless hours she spent alone in the Bunkhouse, Kate dug out the box of yarns and crochet hooks she had stowed away in the trunk of her car. She hurried through her morning routine, found the afghan she had begun some time ago, and spent an hour crocheting before she started dinner. By the time the men came in she was frying steaks and making cream gravy to go with the mashed potatoes. Jake and Charlie never seemed to tire of that menu and always had steaks and other cuts of meat available for her.

"Boy, this neighbor's beef is really tender, isn't it, Charlie?" Jake said at dinner.

"What do you mean, the neighbor's beef? It's the same meat we've been eating all winter." Kate gulped and added, "You *didn't* butcher someone else's cow!"

"It's an old joke among ranchers," Charlie piped up. "Sometimes we tease each other about butchering the neighbor's beef so we don't have to kill one of our own."

Kate wrinkled her nose at the men. "You shouldn't make fun of a greenhorn."

"Greenhorn? What do you know about a greenhorn, Katie?"

"That's what my grandfather called someone who didn't know anything about living on a ranch."

"We don't think you're much of a greenhorn anymore," Jake said.

"I hope that's a compliment."

"It was meant to be," he said easily.

All through clearing the table and doing the dishes, Kate wavered between feeling good about fitting in on the ranch and reminding herself that she hadn't been invited to spend the winter here. Getting to know each other had taken time but it made a lot of difference. She no longer dreaded being around Jake and she had grown terribly fond of Charlie. He had been the buffer she and Jake needed to get along through these last couple of months. Kate wore the long johns under her pajamas that night and left the woolen socks on her feet that cuddled the hot water bottle she slipped into her bed every night. She woke the next morning and realized she had slept through the night without a bad dream. She pondered this, wishing she could stay in the warm bed rather than getting up and into her daily routine.

She spent the bitter cold days keeping the logs on the fire in the fireplace and kindling in the kitchen stoves. Every day the men came in with frost on their beards and eyebrows. They wore heavy sheepskin-lined coats and liners in their overshoes. Their caps and mittens were lined with sheepskin or flannel. In the afternoon after she finished her work and the fires were all supplied with wood, Kate usually curled up in the recliner near the fireplace and continued her crocheting or took up one of the Zane Grey books or other westerns she could easily become engrossed in. Inevitably, Jerry jumped into her lap if he was in the room. She moved her fingers through the cat's sleek fur and scratched his stomach or ears. Sometimes she simply studied the dark gray stripes that were so perfectly configured on his body. She hadn't been out skiing since the week after Christmas because so far the temperature during January had never gotten much above zero.

Kate resisted the temptation to curl up and pull the covers tight around her body. The room was always chilly when she got up in the mornings, but this morning she felt cold to the bone. Today was her wedding anniversary and if David were still alive he would have brought her flowers and they would have gone out to dinner, at least. She would even have agreed to find a babysitter for Jeremy. Right now, the ranch duties awaited her so she didn't dwell long on the significance of the day. She was glad when Jake and Charlie left to do the feeding. It gave her the time she needed to evoke some the fond memories she had of the anniversaries she and David had shared in the past.

When the men came in that afternoon, one glance at Kate let them see that something was wrong.

"Kate, you've been crying," Jake said gently.

She acknowledged him with a tip of her head, her lips pressed tightly together.

"Can we do anything?"

"It's my wedding anniversary," she said. "They say the first year is the hardest with all these special days coming around . . . I just have to get through them."

"Your husband must have been a fine man."

"He was."

Charlie put a hand on her arm and said quietly, "It's tough, I know."

At the table, Jake said grace as he often did these days and added, "Lord, please comfort Kate. We know she misses her family. Amen."

 CHAPTER TWELVE

The winter nights in January seemed to go on forever and Kate often had trouble sleeping for so many hours. Rather than toss and turn restlessly, she sometimes slipped into the living room to sit in front of the fireplace wrapped in the afghan she had finished crocheting. Occasionally she would fall asleep curled up in the recliner. Kate was having one of those sleepless nights so she got out of bed and tiptoed to the fireplace, trying to avoid the floorboards that creaked. On her way she caught sight of the rising moon, which hung low and full in the sky. She drew a quick breath at the sight of it.

Jake came down the steps into the living room and saw Kate go outside through the Dutch door, dressed only in her chenille robe. He set his lamp on the dining room table. From the porch Kate saw the glow from the lamp and knew Jake had come to put logs on the fire.

"What in the world are you doing out here?" he asked from the open doorway.

"Come see—this is so beautiful."

Jake grabbed a large woolen blanket from the back of the sofa and wrapped himself in it before stepping outside. "It's fifty below out here."

Kate held her robe tightly around her body. "I know. The air fairly crackles with the cold, but just look how the moonlight covers the snow. It sparkles."

Jake opened the blanket and folded his arms around Kate, wrapping her up with him. "I have to admit this is something to see. Look at all the frost diamonds out there."

Kate liked his quaint way of describing the glittering snow. Coyotes yipped and howled into the silence.

"Listen to those coyotes. Are they really close to the house?"

"Maybe, but sound carries a long way in this cold."

She turned toward Jake. "Do you think they carry on so because they're hungry?"

"I suppose so but maybe they're just playing." They listened to the wild cacophony.

Jake's warm breath on her neck and his arms around her began to stir feelings she had reserved only for David. Disturbed by the sensual pleasure he aroused in her, she used the sharp cold as an excuse to mumble, "I think we'd better get back in where it's warm."

"As much as I'm enjoying this, you're right. Charlie might have to thaw us both out if we don't get in out of this cold." Jake gave her a gentle hug and unwrapped the blanket to let her go.

Inside, he handed her the blanket and said, "I'll put some wood on the fires and then how about some hot chocolate?"

"Sure." Kate started for the kitchen.

"You sit by the fireplace and I'll make the chocolate." He put a log on the fireplace grate, set the screen in place, and carried the lamp with him into the kitchen.

Kate huddled in the blanket that was still warm from their bodies. She listened while Jake poked kindling in the stove and set a pan of milk on top. He mixed cocoa with some sugar, made a paste with milk, and poured the mixture into the hot milk after he skimmed the film from the top. Jake had watched Kate make hot chocolate in the same way and asked her why she didn't use the pre-mixed powder in the pantry. There was no powder that could get the rich chocolate flavor like her grandmother's technique, Kate had told him.

Jake took two mugs out of the cupboard and dug into the cookie jar for a couple of sweets. He was preparing their hot drink and finding cookies without much thought to what he was doing. His mind was on holding Kate close with both of them captivated by the beautiful moonlit scene.

Jake carried a tray with the mugs and a plate of cookies into the living room. She removed a book from the table between the recliners so he could set the tray down. The flame from the fire was their only source of light, but it was bright enough that Jake decided not to go back to the kitchen to fetch the lamp. He settled into the recliner and took the hot mug in his hand.

"I've never seen the full moon on the snow like that before," Kate said thoughtfully. "It was simply breathtaking."

"You know in Indian cultures, they call the January full moon the Wolf moon because of the howling, hungry wolves. Some call February the Snow moon because snow is usually heaviest then." Jake took a sip of chocolate and added, "We have a lot of Indians in Wyoming. Personally, I think they've always had nature figured out better than the rest of us who want to change it."

Kate smiled. "I think you're right." She sipped her cocoa then added, "But I can't imagine having more snow than we have now." Kate checked herself. "There I go, wanting to change nature."

"See what I mean?" Jake chuckled.

After a few minutes of silence, Kate said, "I see from the pictures of you and your brother in your uniforms that you look so much alike I'm not really sure which one is you."

"I'm the one on the right. You can't tell much by that picture because we had our Air Force caps on, but my hair is some darker than his."

"I remember him as happy-go-lucky."

"And he was usually the one that got us into mischief," Jake grinned. "Mom would yell, 'Jesse,' then figure out who needed a scolding. Of, course, most of the time we both needed one."

"How long were you in the service?"

"Three years."

Kate took a bite of cookie and sipped her chocolate. "Were you together during the war?"

Jake drew in a deep sigh. "No, we were both pilots and both

in Italy but stationed in different areas. We did manage to get together once."

"That's a long time. Your mother must have been terribly worried all that time."

"She was, and it was tough on the ranch with rationing and all. They had their hired man, and Ben who stayed on with us after your grandma sold us the ranch. They hired a few high school boys to get through haying. "

"I guess you flew bombers?"

"B-17s." He glanced her way. "Do you remember a song about coming in on a wing and a prayer?"

"Yes."

"Well, my crew and I did that twice." He gazed into the flames. "We were lucky, though. It was really tough when a plane was shot down. You never knew if the guys died in a crash, became prisoners of war, or what." Jake sat quietly, lost in memories.

Kate stood up and folded her blanket. "Thanks for the cookies and hot chocolate."

Jake got to his feet, too, and set his mug next to hers on the side table. "Leave those," he said, "I'll take them when I turn in. I just want to put another log on."

"I'll see you in the morning then."

"It's two in the morning already, Kate," Jake said. "If you want to sleep in, Charlie and I can manage."

"No doubt I'll wake up as usual. I have this built-in alarm system."

———•———

Kate awoke early and said her rosary, which she did almost every day. She meditated about the turn of events in her life and how overcome with grief she'd get at odd times. The ever-increasing moments of joy she experienced on the ranch were seeping through any resistance she had held in the past. The beauty of the full moon on the glistening snow had been mesmerizing, but being in Jake's arms troubled her because she liked the secure feeling it had given her. It was as if being in these majestic surroundings, Kate was able to mourn her loss more quickly. She knew of others, who had lost a loved one, opting to live a solitary life for a time. She liked seeing the meadows covered with snow and never tired of gazing at the mountains, especially the steep cliffs where the snow wouldn't stick and where pine trees seemed more deep blue than vivid green. The moment when the range took on a rosy hue reflected by the sunset was also a special display of nature that Kate never tired of. So why should she feel ashamed that she loved the isolation of the ranch and enjoyed the company of Jake and Charlie? Wasn't she allowed to get on with her life? *Is it possible to get over the death of people we love so soon?* Of course, she wasn't over their deaths. It was just that their deaths were so final and they were never coming back. And she was alive and had to go on living in a world without them. Kate had been mulling over these thoughts when she heard someone moving around in the kitchen. She got up and dressed quickly in the chilly room.

"Good morning," she said to Jake who was slicing bacon from a slab.

"Good morning," he replied. "Don't look at the thermometer—you might have a heart attack," he kidded her.

"I don't need a thermometer to tell me it's really cold. What is the temperature?"

"Fifty-two below."

"Is this what the rest of January is going to be like?"

"And probably February. March might be better, but the wind in March sends the cold into your bones."

Kate began mixing sourdough batter for pancakes. Charlie came through the outer door and hurried over to the stove to get warm. "Don't go outside today. It's almost too cold for geezers like us."

"Jake told me how cold it is. I'll keep the fires going so we can thaw you out."

"T'ain't funny, Magee," Jake said with a grunt.

"Fibber Magee and Molly was one of my favorite radio programs." Kate hesitated then added, "That's funny."

"What's funny?" Jake asked.

Kate grinned. "I used to listen to the radio sometimes, but I haven't even thought about a radio since I've been here."

Jake took the pancake mixture from her and spooned out the batter onto the hot griddle. "I guess we ought to have a radio out here but the batteries run down too fast."

Kate felt awful that Jake and Charlie had to go out to feed when the temperatures were so frigid, but the livestock had to eat. The day before, they had taken their four-horse teams out to break a new trail from one field to another before they could feed the cattle. They'd fed all the hay in one field and had to move the cattle and feedground to another field where there were more stacks of hay. They had to shovel snow in the stackyard onto the sled and haul it away so they could get the sled close to the stack. Both men had come in with a heavy frost on their beards and eyelashes. She suspected it would be the same today.

Kate was fascinated by the fact that the cattle wouldn't leave the feedground because the snow was too deep off the feed trail. So the cows stayed on the one trail all the time where they knew they would be fed and could get to a waterhole. One day when she had skied out to the feedground, she had seen Jake chop ice out of the big round tank along the fence between two fields. Charlie told her there was a flowing well in that spot but the water froze over every night so taking out the ice was one of their daily chores.

 # Chapter Thirteen

Jake and Charlie had moved the cattle to a field nearer the house so they were in around noon on one unusually warm day in late January. After dinner, Charlie opened the top of the Dutch door and watched Jake head for the barn.

"I wish Jake would sell that horse," Charlie said. "Red is mean and Jake is not going to tame that mean streak out of 'im."

Kate joined Charlie in time to see Jake come out of the barn with a rope, then open a gate to run all the horses into a small round corral. As the horses circled inside the fence, Jake would let one horse at a time back into the bigger corral, careful not to let Red slip through. When there were two horses left, Jake let a big work horse through and tried to shut the gate on Red, but the powerful gelding slammed into the gate and threw Jake back against the pole fence behind him.

"Oooh, that had to hurt," Charlie said through gritted teeth. "We better go see if he's okay."

Kate grabbed a coat and followed Charlie out the door. In the corral, Jake was sitting on the ground, cussing at Red, and holding his left arm tight against his chest. They helped him into the house where Jake sat on the side of the bed, his face pale and tight with pain, while they took off his coat. Kate asked Charlie to pack snow in a plastic bag while she helped Jake take off his shirt and underwear. Jake's eyes were shut tight and he held his breath as Kate and Charlie wrapped the bag of snow around his arm. Kate washed her hands then filled a basin with warm water from the reservoir on the stove. She washed Jake's arm thoroughly with soap, rinsed it well, and sprinkled talcum powder to keep it dry between his arm and chest. Jake told her his head hurt and pointed to the spot.

"You've got a goose egg," she told him. "You're lucky you had that felt cap on or it would have been worse." Kate took his hand and tried to move his fingers.

Jake asked irritably, "What are you doing?"

"Just checking to make sure you have no damage to blood vessels or nerves," she replied as her fingers moved over his hand and wrist.

He insisted that his arm hurt and told her to leave it alone.

"I know it hurts, it's broken. We'll have to splint it."

Stricken by what that meant, he protested, "Look, I need both arms to feed . . ."

"I know that." She went on, "We'll see what we have in David's medical bag to make a splint."

She helped Jake to a chair at the table while Charlie brought the medical bag to the dining room. She gave Jake a painkiller and removed the icy bag from his arm.

"Good, your arm hasn't swollen much."

"That's a good sign, right?" Charlie asked hopefully.

Kate nodded. To Jake she said, "This will hurt but the medicine I gave you should help."

"Just do what you have to do!" Jake snapped.

"Charlie, would you bring me some warm water, please?"

Kate took out some rolls of plaster and measured against his arm the length needed. When she'd made a long pad of the plaster, she dipped it in the water, squeezed out the excess, and ran it from the front of his upper arm down under the elbow and back up the same way on the underside. When it had begun to dry, she asked Charlie to dig out some Ace bandages she could use to wrap around the splint.

Charlie helped Kate clean up everything and told her to sit down and rest while he added kindling to the stove and put the teakettle on for some tea.

"I just need to get a towel to make him a sling."

Jake leaned back against the chair. "Thanks," he said when she sat down.

Charlie set a cup of tea in front of her. "Gosh, Kate, I don't know what we would have done without you." He glanced at Jake and saw that worry lines creased his forehead.

Jake sat staring at the cup of tea. "I've made a real mess of things. I won't be much help carrying this around," he said, pointing to his disabled arm.

Charlie stood up. "Don't worry, Jake. We'll manage. Right now, I'd better milk and get the eggs."

"Just get enough milk to give to the pigs in the morning and turn the calf in. You'll have enough to do in the morning without having to milk too." Jake rubbed his forehead, and sighed. "Sorry, Charlie, I've put a big load on you," he said despairingly.

"We'll get along okay. You just gotta let that arm heal," Charlie told him.

He said he didn't want anything to eat but Kate cajoled Jake into trying some beef broth. "It could have been worse," she said, watching him use the spoon in his right hand.

"How so?" he asked doubtfully.

"It could have been your right arm."

"Yeah, you're right," he conceded.

That evening she checked his head and told Jake that the lump had gone down some.

"Have you had a tetanus shot recently?" she asked.

"Yes. Charlie and I had one just before we moved up here. Manure and rusty nails are bad about giving someone tetanus, you know," he teased.

"You're lucky you didn't get a concussion. That's not to say there couldn't be complications. You'd better get to bed and get some sleep."

Jake tried to convince her that he was all right and she should go on to bed. Kate tried to sleep but got up twice during the night to check on Jake. He woke up each time and studied her face while she took his blood pressure and temperature.

When she finished she leaned to tuck the covers around him and said, "Good night."

He caught her hand and said, "You know, I thanked God for sending us a good cook. I guess I'd better thank Him for sending me a nurse too."

She smiled and said lightly, "He probably should have sent you a doctor—but I'm glad I could help."

He studied the cast on his arm. "You're a wonder," he said solemnly.

He watched her go in the fading glow of the lamp.

Chapter Fourteen

Just before sunup, Kate got out of bed, dressed, and tiptoed into the kitchen to start breakfast. Jake was pumping water into the coffeepot. She set the lamp she was carrying on the counter.

"You should have stayed in bed, it's still dark," Jake said.

"You must be feeling better, but you should have stayed in bed, at least for today."

"Don't fuss, Kate. Aside from a sore shoulder and a little headache—and a useless arm—I'm fine."

They had breakfast ready when Charlie came in. Kate poured their coffee then hurried through her breakfast and began clearing the table before the men were finished. As she poured boiling water from the teakettle over the dishes in the drainer, Jake opened the door to the mudroom.

"Where do you think you're going?" she asked.

"Going out to feed," he answered.

"Oh no you're not! If I'm doctor enough to set that arm, I'm doctor enough to give you orders to stay inside. You can still develop an infection. And we don't need that," she said sternly.

"It's too much for Charlie to do on his own."

"That's why I'm going to help Charlie and you're going to keep the fires going here." She pulled on a pair of ski pants over her woolen pants.

"You're bossy. At least put on another sweater. Better yet, wear this windbreaker over your coat," he said, lifting the jacket from a hook. "The hay won't stick to it." He took his Scotch cap from the shelf. "And wear this too."

She pulled a ski mask down over her head and reached for

her braid. With his good arm, Jake pulled the heavy length of hair from under her coat collar. "I'm just warning you. You might freeze out there."

"Well, I thaw out pretty good," she said with a saucy grin.

"You're sassy too." Jake flinched and put a hand up to the sore spot on his head.

Kate gave him a knowing look and went out the door after Charlie.

"Kate, I can do the feeding. It's too damn cold out here for you," Charlie said when she caught up with him.

"That's the first time I ever heard you swear, Charlie. But you're right, it's damn cold out here." He chuckled.

"Be sure you keep moving, stomp your feet, and swing your arms now and then to keep the blood circulating," he said in a serious tone.

Charlie handed the halter rope to Kate after he harnessed each horse and she led two of them to the sled while he led the other two. Charlie talked softly to the horses as he hitched them to the sled.

It wasn't easy for Kate to climb up on the sled because of all the clothes she had on, but she was standing at the front when Charlie gathered the reins and climbed on.

"I'm glad Jake made me put his cap over my ski mask. It really covers my ears," she said, peering at Charlie through the mask.

"You can't take any chances when it's this cold."

"How come you don't close the gates?" Kate asked when they had gone through a second one.

"There's too much snow . . . and the cows stay on the feedground anyway. They'll be glad to see us coming but they'll wait for us to bring them some hay."

About halfway between the gate and the stackyard, Kate asked, "Why are all those cattle looking in the same direction?"

"They see something. Look over there." Charlie pointed to the northeast.

At first Kate didn't see the dark outlines near the forest edge. She peered out and looked harder. "What are they?"

"Coyotes. They're watching the cows, hoping to catch a weak one that they can kill." Charlie shrugged. "We usually see some around. Food is probably scarce for them now. Sometimes they pounce on a deer or elk that is weak from not finding enough to eat in all this snow. I guess the cows have a better chance 'cause they're all together, they're well fed, and they can chase the coyotes away."

"What about wolves? I haven't seen any—not that I could tell if it was a coyote or a wolf."

"There aren't any. Trappers got rid of wolves years ago because they kill the stock and wildlife too."

When they approached the haystack the lead horses stopped at the gate. "The cows stay on the feedground, but if they found a gate open to the hay they would all be in the stackyard so we have to keep these gates closed," Charlie said.

"I'll open the gate," and she turned to get off the sled.

"No, I'll do it, you just hold the horses." He handed the reins to Kate. "Just keep the reins tight, I'll drive 'em in." He opened the gate, climbed back onto the sled, drove the team through, and deftly guided the horses until the sled was next to the haystack. Then he wrapped the reins around the sled post. The horses stood quietly while Charlie and Kate forked hay onto the sled. Charlie had shed his outer coat and hung it at the front of the sled before he began pitching hay. Before long, Kate took off her heavy coat and wore just the windbreaker.

When the sled was piled high with the loose hay and she was sitting on top, Charlie opened the gate in front of the horses. "Start 'em, Kate, they'll know what to do!"

"Get up," she yelled when she had the reins firmly in her hands. Kate felt the power of the horses as they leaned forward and plodded a few feet before tugging the heavy sled through the gate.

"Whoa, now," Charlie commanded and the horses stopped. He climbed up the back of the sled and worked his way across the load of hay to take the reins from Kate. "Good job, Katie."

"I like this," Kate beamed. "I'm beginning to see what keeps you and Jake so contented."

The process of unloading the hay was a lot easier. Kate helped Charlie pitch the hay off in a steady rhythm while the horses followed the worn-down path of the feedground and the cows rushed to find a place along the hay line. They piled another load of hay onto the sled. They fed that load to the cattle and then put on another load before Charlie closed the gates and they headed for the mangers at the barn. By the time they finished the feeding, Kate was weary but invigorated by the open air, hard work, and seeing the horses follow their routine so patiently.

"You'll be pretty sore by tonight," Charlie said when they reached the barn. "We'll heat up some water so you can have a hot bath."

She drew in an icy breath and admitted that she was beginning to feel the effects of using muscles more strenuously than they had ever been used before. Her arms felt heavy—the soreness would come later, she supposed. By evening she was exhausted and aching even before Charlie had a chance to heat up the water for her bath.

Later on, when she came out of the bathroom, Jake called to her. "Let me put some liniment on those arms."

"What is it?" she asked skeptically.

"Horse liniment," he replied nonchalantly.

"Let me look," she demanded, reaching for the bottle in his hand. When she saw the Absorbine Jr., she knew what it was. "Thanks, I think I need some."

Jake sat down beside her on the bed. With his one good hand, he helped free her arms from the chenille robe. She had on a flannel nightgown but the elastic around the wrists was loose enough to allow him to reach her shoulder.

"I'll hold the bottle," Kate said, realizing it would be difficult for him to hold it in his left hand. He rubbed the liniment up and down her sore arms and onto her shoulders as far as her

sleeves would allow. He slid his hand down the back of her neck
to apply some of the pungent liniment across her shoulders
and upper back. His touch became a caress and Kate let him
continue for a few minutes.

"Whoa, that's enough," she finally said as she put the lid on
the liniment.

Jake sniffed around her earlobe and teased, "What strong
perfume you have, Grandma." Before Kate caught his meaning
he pulled her close and kissed her on the temple.

"Look, you big bad wolf, go find Little Red Riding Hood,"
she said, trying to make light of the intimate moment.

The next morning Kate was ready to go feed again. She had
barely said good morning to Jake when he announced, "Look,
Doctor, I'm going out with Charlie today. You can come along
if you want to."

They banked the fires and Jake insisted she wear his Scotch
cap. He pulled an old one out of the closet for himself. Kate
browned a pot roast and added some vegetables while the men
hitched the teams. Jake helped with harnessing the horses, but
he had to let Charlie open and close the gates. He tried pitching
the hay and grimaced with pain when he moved his broken arm.
It was no use. He grumbled and watched helplessly while Charlie
and Kate worked. They were back in the house earlier since they
only had to feed two loads. The pot roast and vegetables were
tender and just needed heating up. The fire had burned down to
ashes some time before they got in from feeding.

Once as they were unloading hay in a manger for horses,
Charlie pointed to a stout gelding and told Kate that was Red,
the horse that knocked Jake against the fence.

"Red is strong enough to be a work horse but he's too tall
and rangy," Jake said. "Besides, Red wouldn't do anything he
didn't want to do anyway." Kate watched the horse and decided
he definitely had a defiant look.

Feeding the animals became part of Kate's regular routine for the next few weeks. The snow was about three foot deep, giving her the impression they were driving through an open tunnel where the horses and sled runners had worn down a path. Only the tips of fence posts sticking out of the pristine white landscape were visible, and sometimes even those were covered. After every snowstorm, Charlie got out the snowplow to clear the area around the house and barn, even enough so they could pull the sled next to the mangers. But the path from the porch to the gate had to be shoveled and much to Jake's dismay Kate insisted that she could do that.

"I'm so damned useless," Jake said after Kate came in from shoveling the pathway.

"Seems to me you do enough with one arm," she told him.

Charlie added, "We're doing okay and tough as it is, you do a lot."

While the men hitched the horses to the sled, Kate oftentimes put something on the stove to cook slowly. Occasionally she prepared most of a meal for the next day when they finished feeding in the afternoon and Jake helped as much as he could.

For Kate, an unexpected sight was getting a closer look at elk on the hillsides while they were feeding the cattle. She had seen them before but only from the house. From time to time, they spotted a few deer and often saw coyotes. Kate was disappointed that they hadn't seen a moose when they went to feed the cattle. Then one bitterly cold morning, as they were approaching the stackyard, the horses began prancing and tried to turn back. Charlie had his hands full trying to control the horses, and because Kate had been opening and closing the gates since Jake broke his arm she jumped off the sled and put her arm through the gate pole to snug it to the post so the wire would slip off.

"Kate! Get back on the sled . . . now!" she heard Charlie yell.

She had barely pulled her arm back when she saw two moose coming around the far corner of the haystack. The mama moose started toward Kate with ears laid back and fire in her eye. Kate turned and nearly collided with Buster who jumped the fence, streaked toward the moose, and confronted the big animal with ferocious barking. Kate headed toward the sled on a run and Jake reached for her but missed as the horses bolted into the deep snow. Kate grabbed for the sled's angled support pole and managed to hang on until Jake could pull her onto the floor of the sled. As she gasped for breath, Jake stepped to where Charlie was slapping reins against the horses' rumps and calling each to git up and keep going.

Jake yelled, "Push 'em, hard, Charlie. If they stop, we won't get 'em through the snow." Kate looked back and saw that Buster was barking furiously at the heels of the cow moose as she ran around the haystack.

Finally, the teams pulled through to the feed trail and stopped to blow. Jake came back and knelt beside Kate. "Are you okay?"

"I am now but I was sure that moose was going to get me."

"The fence and Buster probably saved you from being hurt," Jake said. "Not only did she not want us in her haystack, she was protecting her calf."

Charlie got the horses settled down and turned toward Kate. "Are you all right, Katie?"

"Yes, I'm okay. But no one I know would believe I almost got trampled by a moose," she said. "How did the horses know the moose were there?" she asked a moment later.

"The horses can sense a moose nearby and probably don't trust them much. Next time, we'll pay more attention to what the horses are trying to tell us."

"I hope there isn't a next time," Kate said. "That was much too close for me."

The cow moose turned on Buster so he gave up the chase and made his way to the sled. Charlie had already suspected what Jake knew—the moose claimed that stack as their own and wouldn't leave until they were good and ready, so he wasn't surprised when Jake said, "We'll have to break open a trail out to that stack." He pointed toward a stackyard back along the trail that was only a few hundred yards off the beaten path.

The horses fought their way through more drifts and Charlie shoveled enough snow to get the sled next to the haystack so they could load the hay. Jake managed to pitch a lot of the hay onto the sled but it was awkward and frustrating. After they fed the cows, Charlie opened the waterhole and they started for the barn.

The fires had to be stoked and the leftovers warmed before they could eat. Three weary humans and one tired dog had a nap as the late afternoon sun waned.

The next day, even though they had to bring a load of hay into the barn, they were in by two o'clock.

Jake followed Kate into the mudroom and slipped his good arm around her shoulder.

"I think you're spoiling the animals around here," he said. "Jerry is always sitting on your lap. Buster practically ignores me, and the horses expect you to nuzzle them while we're hitching them to the sled. You've spoiled that calf to death, too."

"Dickie? You mean Dickie?"

"Who?"

"I named the calf Dickie."

"Oh, yeah, I forgot." Jake grinned and shook his head while Kate unbundled her clothes.

Seeing as they were in early enough, Jake offered to ski out to get the mail. Charlie had been doing that since Jake's arm break and Kate had gone along a couple of times. She would have gone more often but the housework was falling behind from her days away from the house and most of the time she was too tired to ski that far anyway. Jake insisted that he could manage with one ski pole, but Kate decided to go with him and he didn't try to stop her. He let her sling the mailbag over her back and commented on how strong she was getting from the weeks of helping them with the feeding. When they got to the mailbox, Kate told Jake to rest while she put the mail in the bag. The first two letters she pulled out of the box had a return address from Laurie Wagner, Saratoga, Wyoming. It startled her and she felt uncomfortable, almost as if she had seen something she wasn't supposed to. *Were Jake and Laurie getting back together?* She slipped the letters into the bag with the other mail, tied the heavy string, and slipped her arms through the straps as she asked, "Ready?" At the Bunkhouse, she left the bag on a chair in the kitchen. After supper, Jake pulled the mail out of it and hung the bag back on a peg in the mudroom.

—•—

One afternoon near the end of February, when the feeding was done and the men had helped with the dinner dishes, Charlie went to his bedroom to take a nap. Kate stayed in the kitchen to change Jake's splint.

"I bet you and Charlie are as glad as I am to get that smelly thing off," Jake said as she finished washing his arm.

"Oh, so you noticed how we were avoiding you, did you?" she teased.

Afterwards Jake suggested they sit by the fireplace and rest.

Kate chose one of the recliners and took up her crocheting. Jake came in from the den with a book and sat in the other recliner. There was an easy silence between them. She had crocheted a couple of rows when she sat back and glanced over at Jake. His book was open in his lap but he was looking at her. He smiled at her with an unusual tenderness, which unsettled Kate, but his gaze never wavered.

"Good book?" she asked.

"I guess. Can't seem to get into it though."

"Oh? Why not?"

"I don't know."

"Is there something on your mind?"

Jake stroked his beard. "Do you think you'll ever marry again?"

Kate was caught off guard by his question.

"Sorry, I didn't mean to make you uncomfortable, but you're young and have a lot of years ahead of you."

Kate relaxed a bit. "It hasn't been a year since David and Jeremy died in that accident. To marry again would be disloyal—at least for me. I can't even imagine marrying again."

They sat watching the flames.

At last Kate said, "You planned to be married a few months ago and it didn't work out. Have you ever been married?" She thought it strange that a man his age, as good looking as he was, and as settled in his life as he seemed to be, had never married.

Jake replied, "No. I've had girlfriends but never got serious about anyone until Laurie came along. She was more cute than pretty, and I thought she loved me. I could tell, though, that my family and friends thought I was making a mistake. After the wedding was called off, one of my college friends confided that he thought I'd had a narrow escape."

"It seems life is like that. Full of narrow escapes, I mean." The significance of Kate's words weren't lost on Jake.

"My folks live in Arizona these days. Dad can't take the altitude anymore and Mom is pretty crippled with arthritis. But she managed to come for the wedding and she was quite frank about her opinion of Laurie. Right away she said Laurie seemed far too interested in how much land and money this family had. And Laurie told Mary Anne, my sister-in-law, that the house would simply have to be redecorated or torn down and a new one built. Well, that house was Mom's old home there on the Saratoga ranch and it was a beautiful house so when Mom heard that, you can imagine what it did to her opinion of Laurie."

"Rightfully so, I'd say," Kate said.

"Actually, when Mom heard about that she talked to me and I told her that Jesse and I were planning to trade ranches so it wouldn't be a possibility anyway. I assured her that Laurie had better not suggest that we redo or tear down this house. Now that I look back, I can see that Mom was plenty worried that I might give in to Laurie."

The room became quiet, although it was not an uncomfortable silence. Finally, Jake gave a tiny laugh and said, "Several people thought they were comforting me when they said things like 'it's probably for the best.' Wasn't exactly what I wanted to hear at the time but now I can see that marrying Laurie would have been a dreadful mistake." He looked directly at Kate and said, "Even if Laurie had come here, she would never have worked like you do to make this isolated life pleasant."

"I'm glad it's been pleasant for you. I can tell you now I expected that being snowed in here was going to be a miserable winter. But it's so peaceful, and you and Charlie have truly helped me realize that, even though I'll never stop missing David and Jeremy, I can go on without them. I can't change what happened but I don't intend to burden other people by becoming obsessed by my loss. I saw that when I was nursing and it's awfully hard on families and friends."

Jake nodded and then stretched his shoulders and back. "Well, I hear Charlie getting ready for chores. Let's have cold cereal and some fruit for supper."

"That sounds good to me."

"Of course, we could probably eat some of those cookies," Jake added with a wink.

"So you liked them. I'd never put dates in those cookies before."

 ## Chapter Fifteen

One morning when they were on the sled headed for the haystack, Jake knocked on the cast with his good hand and demanded, "When can we take this thing off, Kate?"

"It's only been five weeks. I'll change it again but we can't take it off for another three weeks."

Jake scowled.

"Even then you have to be careful not to damage it by pitching hay right off the bat," she cautioned. "Your arm won't have the muscle tone it had and the bone is still fragile."

Kate heard Jake swear under his breath several times in his frustration at trying to do his share of the work. It didn't help when Kate said that he might be damaging his arm the way he twisted it around with each forkful. He seemed even more irritable as the day drew on and when she suggested they play a game of Scrabble after dinner, he brusquely tossed aside the idea and told her to play with Charlie.

Charlie spoke up, "Good idea, Kate. He's too grumpy and he'd be mad when we beat him."

They played several games before Jake came by the table and told Charlie, "Time to do the chores." Kate made ham and cheese sandwiches for their supper while Jake and Charlie were at the barn. As soon as she cleared the table and washed their few dishes and the milk buckets, she went to her room.

The next afternoon, Jake was in a better mood but still grumbling about his "damn cast." After dinner, Kate was looking through the cookbook she had found in a cupboard. A notation alongside a recipe for ice cream caught her attention.

Jake's mom or someone had written that it was easy to make and delicious.

"Do you make ice cream sometimes?" Kate asked, pointing out the note to Jake.

"Well, yes, Mom used to make it quite often . . . when she could find someone to man the ice cream freezer." ＼

"Well, why don't we try to make some," Kate said.

Charlie piped up, "I tell you what, there are so many icicles hanging on the garage that I could knock 'em down and crush enough ice to fill that bucket."

While Kate mixed the ingredients for a container of ice cream, Jake brought the ice cream freezer and some rock salt from the storeroom. He carried both out to the porch where Charlie was pounding icicles in a gunnysack. Kate washed the can and lid along with the dasher. When she finished, she poured the cream into the can and took it out to Jake. He settled the can over the knob in the bottom of the freezer and fastened the crank over the top, securing it by pushing the thumb lock over the prong on the frame. The men dropped handfuls of ice around the can for a few inches, added some rock salt, more ice, more salt, and continued until only ice covered the lid.

Charlie said, "I'll do the chores while you two finish making the ice cream."

Jake folded a gunnysack on top of the freezer and began turning the crank. "Well, someone is going to have to sit on this freezer. This bad arm can't hold it down, that's for sure."

"I can do that," Kate said and sat down on the freezer. Charlie came out the door with the milk bucket and was nearly to the gate when Kate said, "I haven't thought of ice cream since I left the city. Imagine having a treat like that way out here in the dead of winter."

Jake didn't say anything. She looked around to watch him turn the handle and asked, "Is that hard for you? I could do that part and you sit on the freezer."

Jake grunted. "Nothing is easy with this cast on. It's like

trying to do something with one hand tied down," he grumbled. He kept turning the handle.

Finally, it was becoming harder and harder to turn the dasher in the freezing cream and sometimes the bucket moved a little in spite of her trying to hold it down. "This reminds me of the times I used to sit on the freezer for Grandpa. He sure liked his ice cream," Kate said.

"Your grandparents were special people. They were good neighbors and we all thought a lot of them." He kept cranking the handle then said, "Your folks weren't much help to them on the ranch."

Kate stiffened. She certainly wasn't in the mood to hear another tirade about her parents.

"You don't talk about your mom and dad much," Jake said into the silence.

"So what? You don't talk much about your folks either," Kate replied icily.

"Forget it. I just meant that none of us could figure out why they even came when your granddad got hurt."

She stood up so abruptly that the bucket nearly toppled. She faced him, her hands on her hips, and between clenched teeth she ground out, "Do you honestly think I would ever mention my parents to you again?"

He winced at her harsh words and muttered, "Sorry."

She sat back down on the ice cream bucket and folded her arms. She didn't move or speak until Jake said he couldn't turn it anymore and the ice cream was done. Kate removed the gunnysack and resisted the temptation to slap his hand away when he helped clear the ice from around the top of the freezer. When she had the dasher out and scraped what cream she could from the blades, she put it in a shallow pan and headed for the kitchen, leaving Jake to pack the ice around the can.

It didn't escape Charlie that Jake and Kate avoided any conversation between them at their light supper, while she washed up, and even when Jake brought in logs and put a couple on the grate of the fireplace. When she finished the dishes, Kate excused herself and went off to her room.

Later, Charlie knocked on her door and asked anxiously, "Are you all right, Katie?"

"I'm fine," she reassured him. "I'm just going to bed so I'll see you in the morning." She didn't sleep very well, the room was too cold, and she should have left the door open.

She was in the kitchen before either of the men came in the next morning. She built the fire in the kitchen stove, set coffee to boil, sliced some bacon from the slab, and arranged it in the frying pan. She was mixing pancake batter when Jake appeared.

"Look, Kate . . ."

"Never mind," she said sharply. "I don't need your help."

He closed the door between the kitchen and mudroom and soon she heard the outer door open and shut. Charlie came into the kitchen from the mudroom. Buttoning up his coat he said, "Jake's got the milk bucket. He can't milk a cow yet." He looked at Kate and said, "I don't know what happened between you two but he's like a bear with a sore head."

Kate made a quick decision. "Sit down a minute, Charlie. I want to tell you something."

He sat on the stool at the counter and she stood before him. "You're a dear and I want you to know I think the world of you, but I think I need to leave here."

A stricken look came over Charlie's face but she went on, "I spent every summer with my grandparents until I was sixteen. I think I was eleven or twelve when the McClarys bought this ranch and became their neighbors." She poured some cold water in the boiling coffee then set the coffeepot to the side.

"Did Jake tell you any of this?" she asked.

"Some of it."

"I had a big crush on Jake and followed him around and probably embarrassed him the summer he came to help my grandparents with the haying." She turned the bacon as she talked. "Jake still has a terrible impression of my parents. I know they weren't much help to my grandparents but they were *my parents* and I don't want to hear anymore about what awful people they were." She turned toward Charlie and added, "He started in on them again yesterday afternoon."

"Aw, Kate, that doesn't mean you have to leave. It's still too soon. Jake is cranky about not being able to do anything, is all. He'll get over it."

"Maybe, but it's best that I get away from here."

Charlie got up and said kindly, "Please don't leave. I can tell you Jake has changed his mind about you as a teenager. Give him time, Katie."

He went out to help Jake with the chores and Kate finished making breakfast. After they had all eaten, she hurried with the dishes and was ready when the men had the horses hitched to the sled. The tension that the three of them felt cut through the bitter cold air as they started out to the field to feed the cattle.

———•———

Kate dreaded Jeremy's approaching birthday but consoled herself with the thought that she would be gone by then and would have the day to herself. Kate went to bed soon after dark but she didn't go to sleep right away. She had left the bedroom door closed and the room was frigid. She huddled in the covers and wished she had brought a hot water bottle to bed. She finally fell asleep and had only slept an hour or so when she woke crying out, "No, oh God, no." When she was awake enough to realize what had happened, she lay back exhausted and terribly sad that the nightmares had started again. She hadn't had one for weeks.

There was no use trying to go back to sleep when she was so cold. She put on her robe and slippers and carrying a heavy blanket with her she went to a recliner, curled up in the chair, and tucked the blanket around herself. The heat from the fireplace gradually let her warm up enough to go to sleep.

CHAPTER SIXTEEN

Kate woke up when she heard Jake drop a log onto the grate. He turned from the fire and was startled to see her. Hoping she wasn't still upset, he asked, "Are you cold? Couldn't sleep?" He sat down in the chair next to her.

"I'm warm. The bedroom was cold though."

They sat in uneasy silence for a few moments.

"I'm sorry about yesterday," Jake said. When Kate didn't reply he continued, "I'll leave you alone if that's what you want but I think we ought to talk this out."

"You weren't at all friendly when you saw me at your breakfast table that first morning and then you were furious that I got stuck here with you and Charlie. We've both made the best of these past months, but what's to talk about. There was nothing good about that summer and I made a fool of myself over you."

Jake listened patiently.

She looked straight at Jake. "I've never talked about my parents because your beating me made it clear that you, and maybe everyone else at the ranch, despised my parents and me. What else is there to say about the whole thing?"

Her words fell heavily in the dark room. Jake sat forward with his elbow on his knee holding his head with his good hand. When he finally looked up, he stared into the flames. Miserable and crestfallen, he said, "You felt like that spanking was a beating." It wasn't a question. It was as if he was seeing what happened that day in a different light. "I know I hit you too hard because my hand and arm ached afterward, but I never thought of it as a beating."

Again, the room was silent with only the sound of a log settling lower.

With the elbow of his good arm resting on his knee and his fist against his jaw, Jake sat looking at the floor. At last he said, "Kate, I really am sorry about that day."

Kate tightened the blanket around herself. "I can see that you are but I forgave you long ago. At least I tried to. Grandma taught me that forgiving someone who has hurt us lets us heal. And, drives out the hate," she added on a somber note. "Somehow, after losing my family, I thought that coming back here where my grandparents were always so good to me and I was happier than anywhere else, I could find some peace and comfort. But I'm afraid that seeing you wasn't peaceful or comforting. I've had to work at the forgiving stuff again."

"I hope you can forgive me, Kate. Do you think your grandmother did?"

"Oh, she never knew about that day. She told me about forgiveness when my mother left and I was so bitter. She said I needed to forgive my mother for leaving and telling my dad he could keep the brat. I hated my mother for saying that. Grandma understood, but she kept quoting the Bible where Jesus said not to forgive seven times but seventy times seven, so eventually I knew I had to forgive for my own peace of mind—forgive my mother and you."

"You say your grandmother didn't know about that day?" Jake asked, looking directly at Kate.

"I've never spoken of it until now. I guess because I was so ashamed. Think about it, I was really excited when you asked me to ride part of the way home with you that day. Then you stopped at that secluded spot, put your arm around me, and pretended that you really liked me. You knew I had a terrible crush on you, the good-looking cowboy. I spent a lot of time that summer trying to get you to pay attention to me. So I was thrilled when you sat down next to me and pulled me close. I thought you were teasing when you said you thought I ought to have sixteen swats for my birthday." She paused and said again, "No, I've never told anyone. I was embarrassed, humiliated, and ashamed . . . still am, for that matter."

"I'm the one who should be ashamed, and I am. The other men teased me about how you followed me around, and I only saw you as an immature spoiled kid that I disliked. I figured I was doing everyone a favor—we all thought the three of you were one big burden for your overworked grandmother that summer." He looked at her. "You didn't even tell your mom and dad about what I did to you?"

"No, I've never told anyone," she said again.

"That explains something. After you got on your horse and left that day and I headed for home, I started thinking that I had really messed things up. I hated to go to your grandpa's the next day to help with the haying because I knew that he and your dad would be furious about how I had treated you, and I probably would be told to get off their place. When my folks found out, they would be furious too. I thought that I might have ruined the close friendship between my folks and your grandparents." He paused, remembering. "But nothing happened. When I got to the ranch someone said your horse had fallen with you and you had a broken arm so the three of you left the night before. No one mentioned what I'd done. I thought that was strange but I was so relieved that I didn't ask anyone anything."

Both seemed lost in their own memories. Finally Jake said, "You didn't eat any supper. Are you hungry? I can get you a sandwich or something."

She shook her head. "No, thanks."

"We didn't even try the ice cream. How about some cocoa?" he asked, getting up and heading for the kitchen before Kate even had a chance to reply.

The chocolate tasted good. Kate cradled the mug in her hands.

"Charlie told me that you want to leave. I suppose we could help you catch the mailman and I can't blame you for wanting to get away from me." After a moment, he added softly, "I don't want you to go." He gave her a wry smile. "Charlie would be so mad at me he would go with you. He thinks of you as a daughter."

"I know but . . ."

"There's been a lot of misunderstanding between us. The worst is how I spoke about you and your parents, especially your dad. Your grandparents accepted that their only son was not a rancher so why couldn't I? They always talked about what a wonderful and talented architect he was. When I saw how bad his allergies were, I had to admit it would be tough to work on the ranch but I chose to overlook that and only see that he wasn't much help." A log fell forward so Jake got up and pushed it back on the grate with the poker. "I never heard your grandparents say an unkind thing about your mother and they doted on you."

"Yes, I guess they spoiled me. *And* my dad did too," she added. "He worked so hard and even though he didn't have a lot of time to spend with me, he really loved me. I probably wasn't very lovable."

"I wish I could have seen through the facade you put up then and been able to see the beautiful woman you would become."

"Thank you, that's a kind thing to say."

"I've never forgotten your hair. It's such a beautiful brown color and it falls in soft curls. Even your long braid is pretty."

"I do have to thank my mother for my hair. We both have thick hair with some natural curl, but mine is brown and her hair is almost black."

"I don't know why you liked me. I was such a know-it-all and thought I was so much more mature than you. I wasn't very nice to you even before that day."

Kate wasn't going to argue with that. She was getting sleepy. Jake noticed her head had fallen back so he got up quietly. She stirred.

"Do you want to go back to your room?" he asked.

"No, I'll stay here. It's too cold in there. You go on to bed."

"Kate, tell me you won't leave," Jake said.

"I guess I overreacted." She smiled. "I can't leave anyway until your arm is healed and you can help Charlie dig hay."

"I'd rather watch you and Charlie dig the hay," he said with a grin. "Good night, I hope you can sleep in that chair."

———•———

Kate didn't wake up until she heard someone putting kindling in the kitchen stove. She stood up slowly, stretching from her long night in the recliner. She washed up, got dressed, and went into the kitchen where Jake was stirring up pancake batter.

She stepped close and said, "Let me do that."

Jake looked at her anxiously, "Kate . . ."

She smiled at him and instead of saying anything, she simply put out her hand. He took it and they shook hands.

"I appreciate that," he said softly and they worked together making breakfast.

When Charlie came in, he said, "Well, it's warmer this morning."

Kate wondered if he was talking about the weather or the atmosphere in the room but she suspected it might be both.

They were eating breakfast when Jake suddenly asked, "Why did everyone call you Kitty?" Charlie looked up at her expectantly.

"My name is Kate but my father called me Kitten when I was little. After I outgrew that, he and everyone else called me Kitty. I hated that name so about the time I graduated from high school, I insisted that people call me by my name."

"Well, thank goodness for that. Kitty does not suit you at all," Charlie said. He took a couple of bites and swallowed before he looked up at her with a worried look. "What about Katie?"

"You can certainly call me Katie, Charlie. In fact, I like it when you do." She smiled at him before she took another bite of pancake.

"Could you do me a favor?" Charlie asked.

"Certainly, Charlie. What is it?"

"Well, we only have to feed two loads so we should get in fairly early today and this long hair is bothering me. Do you think you could cut it? I'm going to shave this beard too. Can't stand it any longer."

"I don't know much about cutting hair but I guess I could at least make it shorter. Do we have scissors?"

Jake spoke up, "Mom always cut our hair and she had a hair-cutting kit around here somewhere. It has clippers and all. I'll find it when we come in."

"Okay, this should be quite an adventure."

"Could I have an appointment too?" Jake asked.

"Only if you promise not to grumble about how you look afterward."

"Well, I sure don't want Charlie chopping it off."

"Humph," was Charlie's only comment.

Feeding the cattle went well and it was a shorter day than most so when dinner was over and the dishes done, Jake found the kit and Kate brought a dining room chair into the kitchen while Charlie washed his hair. They decided it was too dark in the kitchen so they moved to the living room where the afternoon sun shone in. Charlie's hair fell into a natural part so Kate set to work, parting off a few strands at a time. She didn't want to have any spot look bare so she cut cautiously, thinking she could go back and cut a bit more if needed. She even managed to manipulate the hand clippers to taper the hair evenly. Jake walked in about the time she handed Charlie a hand mirror to see what he thought.

Charlie quipped, "Did she make me look like a movie star?"

"Yeah, she did. You look just like Gabby Hayes."

"Oh, yeah, I suppose you think she can make you look like John Wayne."

The easy bantering about Jake looking like a shorn sheep with his beard off and him asking Charlie if he needed help shaving his bushy beard went on for a few minutes.

"Looks good, Kate. Thanks a bunch." She untied the homemade cape and brushed the hair from Charlie's neck.

"Next," she said in her most professional tone as she shook out the cape.

Jake sat down and she tied the cape around his neck. "Well, I'll try to leave some of those curls," she said nonchalantly.

Jake grunted, "I don't think John Wayne has curls."

She worried about not cutting too deep on his hair; it was so dark that a clipped out place would really show up but in the end she managed a nice taper on the sides and back. The top lay in soft short curls that were natural to his hair. He studied his reflection in the mirror and turned a bit to show Kate that he was really pleased.

"What did you say you did before you came here?"

Without answering, Kate loosened the cape to brush the hair from his neck and around his collar.

"You could always become a barber," Jake continued.

She winced. "I think I'll stick to nursing."

"Can't say as I'd blame you," Jake replied. He brought a broom and dustpan but let Kate sweep up all the hair. He carried the chair back to the dining room and put the hair cutting kit away. By the time Charlie came back all pale-faced and clean-shaven, it was time to do the chores.

Kate made some roast beef sandwiches for supper. The men joked with Kate about how handsome she had made them look. Later, they played a couple of games of Scrabble.

She had left her bedroom door open that day so her room was warm enough. After warming the bed with a hot water bottle, she had a good night's rest.

Chapter Seventeen

By the first of March the days were growing longer. Jake commented about it one day as he stood looking out the window with a cup of coffee in his hand. "I'm glad we have more daylight. We'll be calving in a couple of weeks." He turned to Kate who was crocheting in one of the overstuffed chairs by the coffee table. "Do you think we can get this cast off soon?"

"Not just yet. I can't take it off too soon and risk damaging your arm again." Worry creased her forehead. "What if I didn't set it straight?" He started to say something but she interrupted, "Besides, I'm afraid you will try to do too much too soon."

Although Kate and Jake were now polite to each other and things had gone well, they had lost the easiness that had grown between them the last few weeks. Each seemed wary of the other. Bringing up the past had been uncomfortable for both of them.

Kate spent a restless night so when she went into the kitchen the morning of the seventh, she barely spoke to Charlie and Jake. Charlie noticed how quiet she was and asked her if she was okay.

She wiped away a tear. "It's my baby's birthday. Another of those bittersweet memories."

Charlie put an arm around her shoulders. "Would you like to stay in today?"

She shook her head. "No. Thank you anyway. I'd rather keep busy."

Before Jake broke his arm, sometimes Kate played the piano
and he strummed his guitar in the evenings. They both sang
and particularly liked the popular western songs they knew so
when the feeding was done, dinner was over, and the dishes
washed and draining that evening, Jake suggested they play and
sing some tunes.

"But you can't play with that cast on your arm."

"You can play. We can sing."

Sometimes Charlie joined in, but mostly he sat quietly and
watched the two younger people. He was thinking that they
made a good-looking couple.

Kate was looking through a stack of sheet music when Jake
said, "How about this one," and picked up "I'm so Lonesome I
Could Cry."

She played the melody and sang along with Jake but when
they got to ". . . as I wonder where you are, I'm so lonesome I could
cry," Kate stopped and took a moment to compose herself.

Charlie stepped up to put his hand on Kate's shoulder.

Jake told her, "Aw, Kate, I'm sorry. I didn't even realize how
sorrowful that song is."

Kate pulled a tissue from her pocket and wiped her eyes and
blew her nose. "It's okay, Jake. I can't stop thinking about Jeremy
today."

Charlie was rubbing her shoulder and said softly, "We know."

Kate shivered. Jake told her, "Go sit by the fire. I'll put the
music away."

Kate opened some canned fruit and set out some cookies
for supper. She brewed hot tea and had all on the table by the
time Jake finished separating the milk and Charlie had washed
up. After supper Kate washed their few dishes and the milk
bucket. Jake and Charlie were visiting in front of the fireplace
when she opened her bedroom door for the night. She fell
asleep long before the men left the living room.

Finally, Kate said the cast could come off but only after she
made Jake promise he would take it easy working up to full use.

"No milking the cow and be careful about pitching hay," she cautioned.

"I know, I know," he told her, holding up his good hand to ward her off.

Kate unwrapped the Ace bandages that had held the splint in place and dropped them into a small paper bag so she could wash them later.

"Sorry," she murmured when he flinched. Some of the splint had stuck to his tender skin but she worked it loose gently and then the whole thing slipped down over his bent elbow.

"Boy, am I glad to get that off," Jake said, testing his arm movement gingerly.

"It'll smell better after a bath," she said, wrinkling her nose.

They both laughed. He pulled her into his arms, hugged her and said, "You're some nurse."

She grinned and told him, "And you're some cowboy."

The next morning and for two days after that, Kate insisted on going along to feed until she was sure that Jake didn't do too much with his arm.

Jake and Charlie rode their horses out to bring the heifers into the small pasture next to the corrals for calving. Kate went ahead of the herd with the teams and sled full of hay to help keep the young cows moving. The first baby calf was born without incident the first night and from then on, the men took turns checking the heifers during the night and often had to pull a calf.

One evening about nine o'clock, Charlie came in to ask Jake for help with a particularly hard birth and Kate asked to go along. Kate held a lantern over the top of the gate and watched anxiously while the men struggled to help the calf through the birth canal. When the heifer was born it was too weak to stand and Kate wanted to cradle it in her arms but the men cautioned that the mother cow was on the fight and even they had to leave the baby lying in the hay and get out of the stall. They all watched as the mother cow licked and nudged the calf but they knew before she did that the calf was dead.

Kate turned to go, her heart heavy with sadness and filled with a sense of kinship with that mother cow losing her baby. Carrying the lantern, she stopped to pet Dickie on the way to the house. He always ran to her as soon as he saw her coming or heard her call to him.

"This is the way it should be—growing and growing," she cooed to her pet. She caressed the soft curly hair and looked into the eyes of the calf. She pressed her cheek to the baby face and stood up to go. She turned to see that Jake was waiting to walk back to the house with her.

"I'm sorry you saw that," he said. "Let's go in, it's cold out here." He held the lantern high enough for her to see the path while they walked the couple hundred yards to the house in silence.

Calving along with feeding all the stock kept the men working all hours. Kate spent her days doing some serious house cleaning since she had neglected much of it during the time she helped with the feeding. Snow began to melt the last few days of March and the first couple of weeks in April. Kate watched water trickling down the ruts in the road one afternoon and although it was frozen the next morning, it was more slush than hard ice and she was encouraged that the snow would be gone before too much longer.

By the end of April, Kate could see the road all along the lane south toward the county road. *It won't be long now until the road dries up.* She planned on keeping in touch with Charlie but she doubted that Jake would write. She hadn't seen any more letters from Laurie or even known if Jake had written back to her, but Kate couldn't help wondering if the romance was rekindling.

Thinking what a beautiful day it was, Kate opened the top of the Dutch door and leaned on the bottom half. Looking out over the ranch yard and sipping a cup of coffee, she found herself quite disheartened that it was almost time to leave the ranch.

She began to think of each weekly household chore as being the last time she would do that in the Bunkhouse. Would she ever churn butter again or make four loaves of bread at a time? Who would wash the windows or clean the storeroom? The ranch had been a haven for her for the long winter months, and driving away would feel like leaving home. She hadn't expected to become so attached to this Bunkhouse, Charlie . . . and even Jake, she had to admit to herself.

As the days grew longer, the men started work earlier in the morning and worked long hours every day. So it came as quite a surprise one early afternoon when Jake came into the kitchen, wearing his cowboy boots and a Stetson hat. Kate had just taken four loaves of bread from the oven.

"I'm going over to the Orland house and see how everything looks after the winter. Would you like to go?"

Kate's eyes widened. "Yes, I think so . . . it's where I was headed when I got my car stuck in the snow."

"Well, I'll saddle a horse for you while you get ready. Better wear your warm boots—those shoes might get all muddy."

By the time Jake led the horses to the yard gate, Kate was just coming out of the house. "This old mare is Candy. We call her that because she is sweet-tempered." Jake handed Kate the reins. She looped them around Candy's neck, held the reins in her left hand as she took hold of the saddle horn, turned the stirrup, put her foot in it, and swung herself into the saddle. Jake grinned. "You're quite the cowgirl. How long since you've ridden?"

He had mounted by the time she answered just loud enough for him to hear. "Actually, you were there."

His smile faded and he wished he hadn't asked.

As they rode, they talked of the weather change and what they might find at the house. Finally he pointed toward the creek. "There's the house."

Kate stopped her horse and stared at the old familiar log house with a barn and sheds around the yard. The longing to be in that old house again overcame her fear that she would break down and cry. They rode on down the hill in silence.

Jake sensed the effect that seeing the old place was having on Kate and decided she probably needed some time to herself. "Why don't you look over the house? I want to check things out and I think there is a bridle here we need."

She dismounted and automatically tied the reins around the top pole of the yard fence.

"Where did you learn how to tie the reins like that?" Jake asked, surprised.

"Grandpa showed me how."

He grinned and turned his horse. "The house isn't locked," he called over his shoulder as he started off on a trot toward the barn.

The house hadn't been used much although Jake had told her that occasionally some of the hay hands stayed there during haying and one man and his wife sometimes stayed on in the fall until the cattle were shipped. She wandered from room to room and recognized a few pieces of old furniture that her grandmother had left there. Wallpaper was peeling in some places and paths through the linoleum were worn thin in most of the house. In the kitchen she pulled open one of two large bins under the counter. They had held twenty-five pound bags of flour and sugar but now it was clear that mice had been in the bins. A few glasses, mugs, plates, and bowls sat on one shelf. A lower cabinet held a couple of rusty cast iron skillets and there was a saucepan with no lid. The old Majestic stove hadn't changed a lot except it was covered with dust.

Kate stepped out onto the porch. Jake was getting on his horse so she got back in the saddle of her horse and waited until Jake came alongside. "Ready to go?" he asked.

She nodded yes.

"Sure you don't want to look around anymore?"

"No, it was good to come but I've seen enough." Seeing the place had convinced her that, without her grandparents, it was no longer hers.

They rode along at a walk most of the time. The horses had to jump a small ditch and both broke into a trot for several yards.

Jake was taking a different trail back, which afforded her a view of the mountains ahead of them to the north. They could see a long way up and down the valley so Kate was enjoying the ride. They reached the hillside where aspen trees grew right down to the meadow and Jake pulled up and got off his horse.

Kate looked around. She stared for a moment at a huge flat rock twenty feet away. "How could you?" she cried. She started to rein her horse to turn away but Jake caught the reins just below the bridle bit and held the horse.

"Please, I didn't mean to scare you," he said. "I just thought this might be the place where we could start over."

She sat on the horse, hardly knowing what to think. She turned toward him and saw the troubled look on Jake's face. He said, "I wish I could undo that day but I can't."

Kate got down and let him tie the horses to a branch.

"Can we sit on that rock?" he asked cautiously.

"I suppose so," she replied, unable to put the picture of the last time they sat there together out of her mind. She walked the short distance with him and sat at the edge of the rock.

There was probably a foot between them when he sat down. He rested his elbows on his knees and held his hands together out in front of him. "Charlie told me the other day that I was a damn fool." He turned to her and said, "He's right, of course. We didn't take care of you this winter; you took care of us. I don't know what we would have done if you hadn't been here to set my arm—and to do my work all that time."

Kate had been watching him and didn't like seeing him so forlorn. "I'm glad I could help. You helped me a lot too, you know."

"I helped you?"

Kate looked out over the meadow. "You remember the night I had such a bad nightmare. That was probably the worst one I ever had, and I've had plenty of them. But I haven't had many since that night and I'm sure it's because you were so kind to let me talk about what happened. It's agony trying to get over losing David and Jeremy but you and Charlie have helped me through the worst months, I think."

"I hope so," Jake said earnestly.

She went on quietly. "Life at home was not much fun. My mother was not very affectionate and I think she was jealous that my father and I were close. But he worked so much that he wasn't around a lot, so as a child my happiest times were here with my grandparents." She stretched her legs and crossed her ankles. "David, Jeremy, and I were a happy family. Life took a dreadful turn but there's no going back." She turned her head and added, "Being on the ranch where I could keep busy has been a great help."

"I'm glad. You kept busy all right."

"Just working for my keep," she said lightly. Jake looked hurt. "I'm teasing." She went on, "I loved keeping the house and cooking for you and Charlie. You always said you liked any meal I made and that made me happy."

"Good. We sure appreciated having a hot meal ready to eat when we got in from feeding."

"And as for the outside work," Kate said, "I only did what I know my grandmother would have done in the same situation. Besides, I enjoyed it . . . after the sore muscles healed."

Just then three deer appeared on the hillside across the meadow. They watched awhile before Jake said, "You know, Kate, it always amazed me how you took that whipping from me . . . what did you call it, a beating?"

"Don't, Jake. I won't call it that again."

"Let's be honest. It was brutal and I will never forget that. Even though I hit you hard, you never cried or yelled or screamed at me. I wondered about that later. After I tossed you on the ground, it seemed hard for you to stand, and even then I wasn't man enough to help you up. You led your horse over to that ditch where it would be easier for you to get on again. I watched you for a long way. Your horse never went so fast as a trot that I could see. I figured that going faster would have been painful after I spanked you."

"You're right about that."

"I've thought a lot about it lately. How could your horse have stumbled going that slow and especially throw you hard enough to break your arm?"

Kate hesitated but finally answered in a low voice, "My horse didn't stumble."

He looked at her with deep furrows in his brow. "Then how did you break your arm?"

She hated to answer that question but there was no way around it. "See that rock just in front of us? That's where my arm broke."

Jake put his hands over his face and groaned. He sounded shaken and miserable when he said, "You mean when I threw you off my lap, you hit that rock hard enough to break your arm?"

"Yes," she said barely above a whisper.

He looked at her with real sorrow. "I am sorry, so sorry. I know now how much you were hurting," he said as he rubbed the place where his arm had been broken.

"It's in the past." Kate patted his arm. "You're right. This is a good place to put all that behind us and be friends." She thought they should leave it at that and start home.

Jake rubbed his forehead. "It must have been an awful blow to realize you were going to be snowed in here with me for several months."

"It was. And you have to admit you were shocked and angry when you realized it was me. When it became obvious that I was stranded, I was afraid of you, but you turned out to be a nice guy." She smiled and looked at her watch. "We should be getting home before the sun goes down."

Jake didn't move. Instead, he took off his hat and turned it around and around in his hands. Finally, he said, "I'm glad we can be friends and I'm glad too that we can put all that past behind us now."

"Do you remember when you said grace and thanked God for sending me here?" she asked.

"I sure do," he chuckled.

"Maybe He did send me here so we could patch things up. It has all been such a bitter memory for me and as for myself, I'm glad to let it all go."

Jake looked directly into Kate's eyes. "You are amazing, Kate. You're kind and generous, you work hard." He paused then added, "And you're a darn good cook."

"And I can beat you at cribbage any day," Kate teased.

They stood up, and without any preamble Jake put his arms around her, hugged her, and whispered, "Thanks for everything . . . and I mean everything."

"Thank you for bringing me here and letting me see Grandma's house," Kate said. "Let's go home."

They'd ridden halfway back to the ranch when Kate turned toward Jake and smiled. "This horse is so gentle. It's a treat to ride again."

"I'm glad," Jake replied, returning her smile.

They rode the rest of the way in silence, both of them lost in their own thoughts.

 **Chapter Eighteen**

There was much to do around the ranch the next few weeks. The snow was going fast by the middle of May and even the road seemed to be drying up. Kate found it hard to deal with the new situation between her and Jake. He remained troubled about causing her broken arm and had mentioned it a couple of times, even though she tried to assure him it didn't matter anymore. She decided it was time for her to leave the ranch, so at supper one night, she asked, "Do you think I could drive my car out now?"

She and Charlie saw the look that passed over Jake's face, but all he said was, "Probably so. But not until we can drive out with you to the highway." He ate a few bites then said, "We've got to butcher a beef. We'll need a roast or something for the branding. In fact, I had better try out the road tomorrow. I'll go over to the Peterson place and see what day would be okay with the neighbors for us to brand."

Kate was puzzled and looked to Charlie for an answer.

"All the neighbors help each other out with the brandings," he explained.

The men butchered a steer the next morning and hung the meat in the meat house. Then Jake drove his pickup out of the garage and headed for the neighbor's house about six miles away. He was back in time for a late dinner and told them right away that their branding day would be the Wednesday of the following week.

"Kate, I've been thinking," he began after they passed the food around and started to eat. "Do you think you could wait to leave until after we brand? I know it's a lot of work to cook for a branding crew. There will probably be fifteen or so that day, but Charlie and I would help you get ready if you'd cook for us that day." He went on casually, "The women always fix a big meal for everyone." Before she could answer he added, "I don't expect you to do it for nothing, I'll pay you."

With a sideways look at Jake, she said, "I wouldn't want any pay. But, what will you tell your neighbors about me? Have you told them I've been living here with you and Charlie all winter? What will they think of me?"

"No, I haven't told anyone, except my mom and dad, that you've been here all winter." He grinned and added, "You can be sure my mom got all the details in the very next letter and actually, she was pleased, especially when I told her you were Kitty."

Kate raised her eyebrows skeptically.

"I'll just tell the neighbors, if they even ask, that you dropped in to see your grandparents' old place as you were going through this country and you agreed to stay on a few days to help out with branding."

"I guess since I never met any of the neighbors except the McClarys, no one will know me. Not that it matters," she said thoughtfully. When she saw that Jake and Charlie were not quite sure about her answer she said, "Sure, I'll cook for your branding crew."

Kate was sitting at the dining room table with paper and pencil the next morning when Jake came in from outside. He wandered over and asked, "What are you doing?"

"I'm trying to decide what to cook. You said you would have meat so I thought roast beef, mashed potatoes and gravy, and canned vegetables. There are two big cans of apples in the storeroom so I could make pies with them." She glanced up from her paper and asked, "Do you want rolls or loaves of bread?

There's still enough yeast for light bread."

"Whichever you want. It all sounds good to me."

"I could make a couple of big Jell-O salads, and we have pickles and olives," Kate said, as much to herself as to him.

"Thanks for doing this." She was so preoccupied that he didn't know if she heard him, so he walked back into the kitchen, pumped a glass of water, drank it, and went back outside.

Kate enjoyed preparing the meal for the crew and she was delighted that a couple of the neighbor women came along to see if they could help with the dinner.

The women accepted Jake's casual introduction and immediately asked Kate what they could do to help. They explained that they didn't know Jake and Charlie had someone to do the cooking so they intended to help the men out. She gave each of the two women something to do with the preparations, then chatted away about living in Kansas for several years and how happy she had been when she had an opportunity to drive by her grandparents' ranch on the way to Jackson where she had a good friend.

Neither of the ladies had known Kate's grandmother very well; she was of the generation of their in-laws, they said. But they did remember that the Orlands had a granddaughter.

Kate was highly complimented by men and women alike for a delicious meal and both women said they hoped to see her again sometime. "You sure know your way around a kitchen," one of them commented as they prepared to leave. The remark didn't escape Jake and Charlie who gave Kate a furtive look, trying not to let big grins come across their faces.

After everyone left, Kate finished putting away the extra dishes and big cooking pots and pans they had used, while the men did the chores. Jake had tried to get Buster to go with him to the barn but Buster laid by the stove in the kitchen until Kate carried a cup of tea into the living room. She picked up her yarn and crochet hook and patted the dog's head before he curled up near her chair.

How strange it had been for Kate to mingle with other people. She hadn't seen another soul except Jake and Charlie for the last six months so the prospect of going out among people now was rather daunting. But she resolved herself to the idea that she needed to move on and have a new start. Her last two letters from Margo had been mostly about Steve. They'd been going together since before Christmas and her feelings for him were sounding more and more serious. To that end, Kate was determined to find her own place to live and not rely on Margo for very long.

Later, when Kate was preparing for bed, her room was quite cool so she decided to sit by the fireplace to brush her hair. She had her head down and was brushing from the nape of her neck down over her head and hadn't heard Jake come into the room until he spoke.

"Kate, what you did today for the branding crew was better than I've ever had it."

Sitting up straight, she smoothed her hair back in place and told him, "I enjoyed meeting everyone and the ladies were a great help, but it felt odd to be with other people besides you and Charlie." She began brushing her hair again.

"Can I do that for you?" Jake asked.

"If you'd like to," she answered hesitantly.

Jake brought a footstool from the center of the room. "Here, sit on this and I'll sit on the fireplace bench." He brushed gently but firmly while the fingers of his other hand pulled through the lustrous strands. He brushed Kate's hair for quite a while.

"I'm sure that must be two hundred strokes," she said finally.

"What, have you been counting?"

"Grandma would insist on at least a hundred, especially when she knew I wanted to quit." Kate reached up to take the brush from Jake. "Thank you, that felt good." Then as an aside, she jokingly asked, "Have you ever thought of quitting this ranch life and becoming a hair stylist?"

Jake pulled the footstool from underneath Kate and caught her before she landed on the floor. Gently he lifted her to her feet. "I'll fix breakfast," he announced. "We're going to have Rocky Mountain Oysters."

She laughed out loud. "Thought you had me there, didn't you? Grandma told me about Rocky Mountain Oysters a long time ago—in fact, I really liked them. But," she said, glaring at him, "I'm not about to cook them." It was his turn to laugh at her. She grinned and went toward the bedroom.

———•———

The next day, Kate started packing and putting things into her car. Jake and Charlie were moving some cattle and didn't come in for dinner until after two o'clock. Nothing had been said about her leaving until they were eating and Jake asked, "Do you need help getting your car packed?"

"I have most everything done already, just some last minute things," she answered.

"If you're sure you want to go, we'll go with you tomorrow," he said quietly. "Would you mind making a list of the groceries that Charlie and I need to get in town?"

No one seemed to know what to say at breakfast the next morning. Kate insisted on washing the dishes and separator before she left. In the meantime, Jake and Charlie drove her car and Jake's pickup out of the garage and Jake took his to the tank next to the shed and filled the truck with gas. Then he filled up Kate's tank even though it wasn't so low on gas and could have gotten her all the way to Jackson.

Right before it was time to leave, Kate went into her bedroom to get the cosmetic bag she had left on the dresser. She glanced around to make sure she wasn't leaving anything else behind. On the nightstand she spotted a family picture of her, David, and Jeremy. Before picking it up, she studied it a moment and felt unfaithful to be wishing she could stay at the Bunkhouse . . . wishing Jake would ask her once again not to go.

Outside, Kate asked Charlie if he would drive her car. She was sure that if she was by herself, she would cry all the way to town and she didn't want either Jake or Charlie to see that. When they pulled away from the house, she looked back to see the shingle on the front porch. "I really hate to leave the Bunkhouse," she told Charlie, sadly.

Charlie pursed his lips and she expected him to say something, but he was unusually quiet. Aside from comments about the weather or seeing antelope and deer, as well as some birds, neither of them had much to say on the way to town. It wasn't until they reached Pinedale that Charlie said, "I'm sure going to miss you, Katie."

Kate placed her hand over his on the steering wheel. "I'm going to miss you too, Charlie. Maybe when I get settled in Jackson you'll come to see me sometime."

"Make sure you write and let me know where you are."

"I will."

"For the record, I'll be there whenever you need me to be. I know it takes a long time to get over losing someone you love so much. I only lost Martha and you lost two in your life but I know how it hurts."

Before long, Jake pulled into a side street and stopped in front of a restaurant. Charlie parked next to him and Jake stepped out of the pickup by Kate's side window. He opened her door and said, "Let's eat before you go on. This is a great place for some chow and you don't need to cook it."

They all tried to keep a conversation going during their meal but Kate was feeling so low that she could hardly add much to what was said. When they reached the car Charlie turned to Kate and said, "Come back to see us." She was too overcome to answer him. He hugged her tight and hurried away to the other side of the pickup.

Kate and Jake embraced. He said, "Thanks for everything. You've really spoiled us. You're always welcome at the ranch so come back when you can." He opened her door and cautioned, "Be careful going to Jackson. It's a good road, but tourists will be traveling to and from Jackson and Yellowstone by now."

"I'll be careful," she replied as she turned the key in the ignition. They both smiled and he shut the door.

Kate had driven several miles when she saw a station coming up and the sign said it was an inn. She stopped, found a phone, and tried to call Margo. Since there was no answer, Kate decided to spend the night at the lodge and try to catch Margo after she got off work the next day. Kate tried to read but she couldn't keep her mind on the magazine. Finally, she lay down and turned off the light. A few tears trickled from her eye before she turned over. The irony of feeling lonely now that she was back to the outside world both amused and saddened her. The ranch had been a little world for the three of them for months. She could see that this new life was going to take some getting used to.

 **CHAPTER NINETEEN**

Kate reached Margo on the telephone early the next morning and they arranged to meet at the hospital when Margo finished her shift that afternoon.

"It's so good to see you, Kate. You've got to tell me all about being snowed in at that ranch," she rambled on as they approached their cars. "You can follow me to my apartment, it's not far."

They were relaxing after dinner that evening when Margo asked Kate if she had cabin fever while she was snowed in all winter. "I know I would have gone crazy being cooped up like that."

"Not at all," Kate said. "The people there became good friends. I had time to read, crochet, cross-country ski, and help with the meals and cleaning."

Half expecting Margo to inquire more about the people at the ranch, she was relieved when Margo changed the subject to Steve and their upcoming marriage. Kate soon realized that Margo's plans were about all she could talk about and that suited Kate just fine.

"I'm anxious for you to meet Steve," Margo said. "He's from Washington but he worked on the ski patrol here this past winter. Since my parents live in Oregon, we'll be married there. I hope you'll be able to come." She paused a minute and said, "We'll be living in Washington so this apartment will be empty. Do you think you want to rent it? A nurse at the hospital asked about it but I could tell her it's taken."

"No, you don't need to do that. I'll look for something in the next few days, and then I'll decide if this is where I want to settle down." Privately, she wanted something with a better view than Margo's place afforded. "If I like it here, I'll apply for a nursing job."

"You won't have any trouble finding a job. They always need nurses here, either at the hospital or for one of the doctors."

They talked about some of their nursing school friends that they had heard from at Christmas. Before long Margo excused herself and went to bed since she had to work the next morning. With Margo moving away from Jackson, Kate understood that she and Margo, good friends that they were, would have only their nurses' training in common and would undoubtedly grow apart. Jackson was probably a friendly town and Kate would make other friends, but it troubled her to think that she and Margo wouldn't be as close as they'd been in the past.

In the morning, Kate scanned the rentals listed in the paper. She found several that sounded interesting but decided she would rather visit a real estate office and let someone else find what she was looking for. Going from place to place and having to tell prospective landlords that she wasn't interested in their apartment wasn't an ideal approach for her. Kate found a real estate office that appealed to her and went there. She liked Mrs. Dailey, a smartly dressed woman with pretty dark hair coiled into a neat French braid. She asked Kate what type of place she wanted.

"I want something with a view—of the Tetons if possible—so it may need to be on a second floor. A one-bedroom would be adequate, with central heating and air-conditioning."

"Central heating is standard but you won't need air-conditioning," Mrs. Dailey assured her.

"Really?" Kate asked in amazement.

"Our summers are not all that hot. Honestly, I don't know of any houses or apartments that have air-conditioning. A good fan is all you need."

Kate could hardly believe it.

"Would you consider a small house?" Mrs. Dailey asked.

"I would, but I'm only interested in renting until I decide if I want to live here permanently," Kate replied.

"I'll see what I can find and call you," she said as they shook hands.

That evening Margo asked how her day had gone and Kate told her she had found the perfect person to find her a place to live.

"Yes, she will do her best for you. I know Anne Dailey and she's well liked around here." The phone rang and Margo spent the next thirty minutes talking to her fiancé.

It wasn't long before Mrs. Dailey had two apartments to show Kate. The first was okay but when Kate saw the second, she knew that was the right one. "I'll take it," she told the agent.

"It's quite a lot more money," Mrs. Dailey ventured.

When she heard the price, Kate reassured Mrs. Dailey that she still wanted it and she would be able to pay the rent without any trouble.

During the three days before moving in, Kate went shopping for a three-piece set of living room furniture with two end tables and matching lamps that adequately filled up the room. She bought a single bed, a dresser, and a chest of drawers in dark oak, and chose rose and green accessories to complement the wood. Then she arranged for the delivery of all the furniture on the same day. She found linens, towels, and new kitchen small appliances and asked to have them delivered too. She'd brought along her own stoneware and silverware. She decided to see how the apartment looked before she bought any pictures or mirrors.

Margo's day off coincided with Kate's move-in date so the two of them had fun decorating and doing more shopping. Finally, satisfied that everything was just as she wanted, Kate prepared a chicken and broccoli casserole, a tossed salad, and a lovely table for their evening meal. Over a glass of wine, Margo said wistfully, "I'm sorry I'm leaving just as you've gotten here. I was hoping we could do some fun things together."

"You and Steve can come to visit anytime."

"You are coming to the wedding, Kate?"

"Yes, I'll book a flight to the wedding. If I find a job before then, I'll tell them I can't begin work until I get back."

Margo left the next week for Oregon and Kate made some inquiries about a job, careful to let any prospective employers know that she couldn't start until after she returned from the wedding. She had plenty of offers and finally settled on nursing at the hospital. She declined a position in the emergency room and another in the maternity ward, knowing that either one would bring back too many painful memories. The supervisor asked her to start as soon as she got back from Oregon because a couple of nurses had vacation time scheduled. That suited Kate who wanted work to keep her mind busy.

The wedding was a delightful affair. Margo was a beautiful bride standing next to Steve, a tall, handsome, sandy-haired athletic man. The ceremony was bittersweet for Kate, but she managed not to shed any tears. She went back to her motel room minutes after the happy couple left the reception. She spent the night and caught a morning flight back to Idaho Falls where she had left her car at the airport. By the time she reached Jackson she was glad for some time to herself. She had been reclusive for so many months that being around a lot of people wore her out.

Kate had only two days to rest and to explore some of the spectacular scenery around Jackson Hole before she started work in the hospital. It would, she reminded herself, have been more enjoyable if she hadn't been alone. She was standing by her car on a flat mesa where she had full view of the majestic Teton Mountains when the vivid memory of her and Jake looking at the full moon came to mind. Now, she could almost relive being wrapped in his arms and feeling his warm breath on her neck. That had stirred a longing to be held by the man she loved. It gave her pause to realize that the man she envisioned was Jake, not her beloved David.

The nurses welcomed her warmly and immediately Kate knew she would enjoy working with them. The supervisor was about her age and Kate liked her from the start. Beginning a new job kept her mind occupied with doing her duties and getting to know the doctors, nurses, and other personnel. She enjoyed her work but there were long hours at home without much to occupy her time. She visited the library several times. Sometimes she could get into a story but oftentimes she found her mind wandering. She spent a lot of time thinking about Jake and Charlie.

Kate was glad to be working the first week in July. She didn't want a lot of time to brood over the one-year anniversary of David and Jeremy's fatal accident. It turned out that she had an exceptionally busy day on the fifth. There had been a number of accidents over the holiday so she had little time to think about the lonely night ahead of her. She was putting notes in a chart when she heard the nurse behind her say "May I help you?"

"Thanks, but I'm here to see Kate."

It was the unmistakable voice of Jake who was standing on the other side of the counter. Kate's heart missed a beat or two as she turned around and saw him watching her.

"Jake, what are you doing here?" she asked, surprised to see him.

"Looking for you," he replied simply.

"Just a minute. I'm almost finished here and then my shift is over."

"I know, I asked."

Smiling, Kate hurried to finish her notes. She put the chart away and said, "I'll be right back." She returned a couple of minutes later with her jacket and purse.

They started down the hall and Jake said, "I was hoping you'd have supper with me."

Kate giggled.

"What's so funny about that?"

"Oh, just the way you and Charlie call the noon meal dinner and the evening meal supper. My mother and my husband's family always said lunch and dinner. I prefer dinner and supper like on the ranch."

"Good. So are we going to supper?"

Kate was bursting with happiness, not only about supper but because Jake had come all this way to see her. "Supper sounds wonderful. Why don't you follow me home so I can get ready?"

"Sure, just remember you're going out with an old cowboy so don't get too fancy."

When they reached the apartment house and parked their cars, Kate invited Jake to come in and wait for her. She poured him a glass of iced tea before she went to shower and change.

About twenty minutes later she came out dressed in Levi's and a long-sleeved rose-colored shirt with the squash blossom necklace resting on her chest. She had taken out the braid and her hair was pulled up on the sides and fastened on top with a silver clip to let the long silky strands fall down her back. "How do you like my new boots?" she asked, pulling up a pant leg. The appreciative look he gave her pleased Kate a lot.

"I like those boots . . . and the rest of the picture too."

Kate was glad to hear him say that but was cautious not to appear too ecstatic.

"It's a little early for supper so I thought we might have a drink first. Okay with you?" Jake asked as he set the empty glass on the counter.

"I'd like that."

They drove over to the Wort Hotel lounge and ordered drinks. When the drinks came, Jake raised his glass in a toast to Kate.

"Is your arm okay?" she asked. "I was so afraid I might not have set it right."

"Sure," he said and flexed it to show her how well it worked. He lifted his glass again and she clinked hers to his. "To my favorite nurse," Jake offered.

"And to my favorite patient." They grinned and took a sip.

"You asked me what I was doing here when I first saw you at the hospital. I couldn't really tell you then but now I can. I came because I knew this would be a hard day for you and I didn't want you to be alone."

Tears welled up in Kate's eyes. She pulled out a tissue and dabbed at them. She composed herself and said, "Since you're here, there is something I'd like to do tonight."

Jake was intrigued. "Will you tell me what it is or is it a surprise? I know how much you like surprises," he said trying to lighten up the conversation.

Kate made a face. "There's a rodeo here nearly every night and I have wanted to go to one, but not alone."

"Well, then, let's take these drinks in with us and get to eating so we won't be late for the rodeo." As they walked to the dining room Jake told her he was so glad she had suggested it. "Like most everyone in Wyoming, I love rodeos."

They ordered steaks and had an excellent meal. They declined dessert but chatted over coffee. Kate had asked about Charlie earlier but now she wondered who was ahead with their cribbage games.

"Oh, we don't keep track. He wins sometimes and I win sometimes. Actually, we're too busy now to play cards. I can tell you one thing, Charlie misses you. He got pretty fond of you over the winter. I hope you'll drive out sometime and pay us a visit."

Suddenly, he said seriously, "Kate, speaking of pay, I never even offered to pay you for all the work you did at the ranch and for us. I said I'd pay you for cooking for the branding crew and I forgot. I'd like to now." He pulled his checkbook from his back pocket and reached for a pen in his shirt pocket.

"Put that away. That wasn't in the bargain and I don't need the money. Those months on the ranch gave me more than money can buy."

His gaze lingered on her face and she suspected he was wondering exactly what she meant by that.

Finally, she said, "Let's walk around the square before we go to the rodeo."

———

"Good idea." He paid the check and as they walked out she slipped her hand in his. "Have you made a lot of friends?" Jake asked.

"Only the people I work with and I've met a few others at church. Margo was here the first couple of weeks but she's moved to Washington to live with her new husband so I'm pretty much on my own." She smiled up at him. "I think I've become a loner. I can't seem to get used to having so many people around."

"I know what you mean."

Jake grew sober. "Speaking of church, you might like to know that I went to see the priest in Rock Springs a couple of weeks ago."

She looked up at him, anticipating more.

"I nearly always went to Mass when I lived in Saratoga but since I moved to the McClary place, I haven't been attending Mass. As you know better than anyone, I really needed to go to Confession, and not just because I've missed Mass." He glanced at her. "So I did."

"I'm glad, Jake." She was thoughtful and stopped in front of a shop window. She turned to face him, held his hands, and said firmly, "Now, let's take the bandages off all the wounds—yours and mine—and declare them completely healed."

Both hands tightened on hers. "No scars?"

"No scars. Let's go to the rodeo."

"Yeah, let's rodeo," Jake said, giving her a heartwarming smile.

They enjoyed the rodeo, especially watching a couple of bareback riders that Jake knew. Afterward, they found a café open and had some pie and ice cream. Jake leaned toward her when they finished and whispered, "Not as good as yours."

"I miss making dessert for you and Charlie. Let Charlie know, will you? You're not going back to the ranch tonight, are you?"

"No, I have a room at the Wort but I'm leaving early in the morning. We have to move some cows tomorrow."

"And I have to go to work early too," she said.

When they reached her apartment, Jake turned to her and said, "Kate, I hope you don't mind that I came today."

"No, oh no, I'm so glad you did. I fully expected to go straight home from work, mope around and feel sorry for myself, then cry myself to sleep." She put a hand on his arm. "You made it a good day for me after all. Thanks."

He reached for her and she went willingly into his arms and returned the kiss he gave her. He held her close. "Will you be okay?" he asked.

She felt like David was watching her and smiling as she told Jake, "I don't know what I would have done without you tonight. I have something pleasant to think about so who knows, maybe I can pack away the sad memories."

Jake kissed her lightly on the lips and walked away. She shut the door and stood against it for several minutes. What a kind and thoughtful thing to do, she mused.

Chapter Twenty

With renewed determination, Kate felt that she could face up to her trepidation when she was asked to work in the emergency room on one of her days off.

A cowboy she got to know as Walt was admitted to the hospital on that day, about a week after Jake left. Kate took care of him and took him to the x-ray department. He'd had what he called a "horse wreck."

"Why can't you be my nurse?" he asked Kate when she was about to leave him in his room.

"I'm sorry. I have to get back to the emergency room. But I'll check on you after my shift is over." She teased, "Was your horse hurt in that wreck?"

"Actually, I think my horse laughed after he bucked me off."

With a cheery smile, she told him to be careful with his broken ribs.

———•———

Kate was glad to be busy but she missed the ranch and Jake and Charlie. She sat down to write a letter to Jake. She considered telling him she was thinking of driving out to the ranch on her next two days off but in the end she settled for a short note to thank him for coming and for being so thoughtful when he knew it would be a bad day for her.

It was a week before a letter came from him. She didn't read it until she had taken off her uniform and shoes, changed into jeans and a shirtwaist, and had a cup of hot tea brewed. Making herself comfortable on the sofa, she began to read. He said he had enjoyed their supper, the walk, and the rodeo and hoped they could do it again sometime. The rest of the letter went into detail about the ranch work and getting everything ready for haying. He said he was trying to line up enough men to make a hay crew. A man and his wife who always helped Jesse had arrived a couple of days ago. He would do the field work and his wife would do the cooking.

Kate stopped reading. *What's this, someone else is cooking in my kitchen.* She was quite surprised at how that hurt. She looked down at the letter. *Of course, it isn't my kitchen.*

At the end, Jake wrote that Charlie was fine but complained that they had lost their good cook and wished Kate would come home. The letter was signed, "Love, Jake."

Kate dropped the letter in her lap. It was so impersonal and disappointing. She reread the last bit. *Did Charlie wish she would come home or did Jake say that?* In the end, she concluded that it was Charlie. She sat drinking the tea and decided to go for a drive. Something was nagging at her and she needed to figure out what it was.

In her exploring around Jackson Hole, her favorite place was the mesa below the Tetons, where she could study the nooks and crannies of those awesome mountains, let her eye follow the twists and turns of the Snake River winding through trees and willows along the valley, and contrast all that with the sagebrush plain where she parked her car. She headed for that spot and pulled into the same overlook where she had been several times before. However, this time she didn't dwell on the beauty, she needed to let her mind open to God and ask Him to speak to her heart. She sat quietly and the answer was clear when it came. The one-year anniversary of David and Jeremy's deaths had so shadowed the weeks and months before the day actually came that she hadn't been able to let go of the pain it would bring. Now that it had passed, she needed to leave it behind with the things that would never change. The strange thing, she thought, was that letting go just happened on its own, or maybe God took it away. Whatever, a great weight lifted from her shoulders while she sat there until the setting sun lit the clouds with fire and set the mountains into an outline along the horizon. She drove back to her apartment and ate her supper.

During her break the next morning, Kate slipped down to Walt's room to check on him. His eyes lit up when he saw her and he reached for her hand. "I was afraid you wouldn't come back."

She didn't stay long, but it was long enough for him to tell her that he had heard she was a widow. He asked if he could take her to supper when he got out of the hospital. Kate told him as gently as she could that she couldn't go out with him because she had lost her husband and didn't really want to date anyone.

"Keep getting well . . . and stay off the next wild horse," she said as she left his room before he could protest.

Summer meant tourist season in Jackson Hole so there were all kinds of entertainment going on and even though Kate tried a few times to take in some of the activities, it wasn't much fun going by herself. She didn't mind going to movies alone so that and going to church were pretty much the only ventures she made in her off work hours. She considered driving out to the ranch the one day she had off in the next two weeks but knew the men were so busy haying that she wouldn't see them anyway.

She found herself being called on to fill in for other nurses who had family emergencies or vacations planned. While being busy kept her from dwelling on her loneliness, there were still too many empty hours in her days and nights. A letter from Charlie related that haying season was going okay. "She isn't the cook you are," Charlie commented when he wrote that they had someone to work in the house. He told her about the horses they had to gentle down enough to use on the hay machinery. They had three young boys and an older fellow driving the rakes and sweeps and, he wrote, "A strong fellow in his late twenties does the stacking. I drive the plunger so I use Pete and Dan (you know how gentle they are). Jake and a college student drive the mowers. Jake grinds the sickles so he has to do that at night."

She only received one other letter from Jake. He said his father was in the nursing home in Arizona and his mother hadn't been well. Jesse, Mary Anne, and the kids had been up one weekend. He also wrote about haying season and how busy they would be for the next several weeks. He had reminded her to come see them and signed off, "Love, Jake."

Kate didn't hear from either of the men until a letter came from Jake the first week of September. Back at her apartment she made herself wait until she could sit down with a cup of tea and savor reading his letter.

After the usual "How are you? We're fine, glad to be done haying and have everyone gone again," Jake wrote, "We'll be bringing the cattle down from the mountains in about three weeks, and I thought maybe you'd like to ride along." Kate closed her eyes and savored the moment. "Oh yes, I would," she said out loud.

He went on, saying he hoped it wouldn't be too cold by then and that a cattle buyer had been to see him and the price he offered was a good one so he had already contracted to sell the calves. "Let me know if you would like to help with the roundup and I'll let you know when it's time to go."

She mailed a letter back to him the next day to tell him she would like to go on the roundup and asked him to let her know early enough that she could arrange to have those days off. But when she hadn't heard from him a week later, she was feeling desolate. She knew they had mail delivered twice a week during the summer so he surely had gotten her letter.

Consequently, it was a shock to see Jake outside the cafeteria at the hospital when she went down to lunch on Tuesday. "Well, this is a surprise. I hope you're not here for a medical reason?" she asked anxiously.

"Hi, Kate. Actually I thought maybe we could go to the rodeo tonight."

She grinned at him and said nothing would please her more.

After they had lunch, Jake said, "I'd like to take you to supper.

I have some shopping to do. If it's okay with you, I'll pick you up at your apartment soon after three."

"I'll be ready. Right now, I need to get back to work so I'll see you later." She watched him walk down the hall until he turned the corner toward the front door.

He was waiting when she finished her shift. After she'd changed to Levi's, a pale pink shirt, leather vest, and boots, she suggested they take a drive up Teton Pass before supper. On the way back, Jake teased Kate a bit about becoming a true western cowgirl. "I suppose now you're going to be wanting a horse . . . with a saddle, of course."

"I wish," she sighed wistfully.

"We'll have to see what we can do about that," Jake said. "But now, just enjoy the view out there. I'd better keep my eyes on this winding road down the pass."

Later, when they'd given their order for supper, Jake caught her hand and said quietly, "Kate, I didn't really come to go to the rodeo, although I want to do that too."

Kate didn't know what was coming but she could tell Jake had something serious on his mind.

"I'll talk to you about it after we eat," was all he said.

The waitress set their plates down and asked if she could do anything else. When they had assured her everything was fine, Jake set about eating in the hurried way he had while Kate could hardly keep her mind on her supper. Their small talk just caused her more anxiety and she was relieved when he stood, picked up the check, and offered a hand to help her up.

He hadn't given her a clue about what he had to say so she was all nerves by the time he sat down on the couch in her apartment and patted the cushion next to him.

"Jake, I'm dying with curiosity!" she said when she sat down.

He took her hand.

"The rodeo was an excuse. I came because I am asking you to marry me."

Kate stared at him a few moments and then looked down.

He worried about what she was thinking. "Kate, I love you very much. I can't think of anything but you." His hand tightened on hers. "I wanted to ask you when I was here before but that wasn't the right time for obvious reasons."

Finally, she spoke. "I've missed you, Jake. I know that. But is it love I feel for you or a longing for more of the companionship we developed over the winter?"

He sat quietly while she struggled with what this meant to her future.

"I love nursing. I'd have to give that up." She touched the arm she set for him and gave a little laugh, "Well, not entirely," she joked. "But I don't want to do something like that again."

"Well, I'll try not to break any more bones," he said lightly. "I do know your work is important to you. I guess I just can't see my future without you." He leaned over and put his forehead against her hair.

"Oh dear," she said uncertainly. "Jake, I've got to have some time to think about this."

"You once told me you could never marry again and I know you meant it then. But, Kate, that was before we got to know each other. To tell you the truth, I was quite disappointed when you told me that. I wasn't thinking about marriage for us but I was discovering what wonderful qualities you have. You're beautiful and I knew there would be men who . . ."

"Jake, you're embarrassing me." She looked at him and said sincerely, "I discovered some wonderful qualities in you too."

They sat quietly with his arm holding her close until he said they'd better go to the rodeo. They had a good time but Kate could hardly keep her mind on what was happening.

At her door he said, "I'd better be going. It's a long way home."

"Jake," she began.

He put a finger to her lips and said softly, "Think about it. Just know that I love you." He grinned and added playfully, "And don't forget that Charlie isn't as good a cook as you are, the house is a mess, and I had to churn the butter the other day."

"Oh, go on. You can hire a cook and a housekeeper. Of course, you might have to pay the next one," she returned his teasing.

She turned serious. "I'm overwhelmed, and honored."

Their kiss left them breathless and aware of what could be. "I hate to leave you," he told her at the door. She smiled and closed her eyes for a moment. And then he was gone.

——— • ———

Kate could hardly keep her mind on her work. She lost sleep and couldn't eat. *Can I give up nursing? Would I resent Jake if long winters began to be depressing? Would I compare him to David? Do I want more children?* Instinctively she knew she wanted children but she wasn't so certain about the other questions that troubled her. At her apartment Monday evening she paced the floor restlessly, wondering if nursing could possibly be more important than a husband, home, and family and telling herself that last winter certainly hadn't made her depressed.

At the ranch, Charlie hoped Jake would tell him what was on his mind. Instead, Jake stared out the window or seemed preoccupied while they worked. It crossed Charlie's mind that maybe Jake was sick. After all, he'd gone to Jackson, maybe to see a doctor. Jake had rushed out to get the mail on Friday and only commented, "Wasn't worth going after," when he came into the kitchen and tossed the mail on the counter.

It had been a week since Jake asked her to marry him and she was feeling pretty low at work thinking about what to do—give up her career or give up Jake and the life he offered her. She had the next two days off, so maybe if she drove out to the ranch she'd know the right answer. One thing was becoming much clearer. Since he had declared his love for her, she was discovering that she loved him too, as well as the life he offered. Before she had made up her mind to go to the ranch the next morning, she walked up to the nurses' station about twelve-thirty Tuesday afternoon and saw Charlie waiting there for her.

"Oh, Charlie, I'm so glad to see you!" she exclaimed, clasping his hand in both of hers. She would have hugged him then and there except for the nurses and a doctor who were at the station.

It was time for her lunch break so she asked Charlie to have lunch with her in the cafeteria.

She had hardly taken her seat when she asked, "How's Jake?" then realized how anxious it must have sounded.

Charlie fiddled with his fork for a few seconds. "Jake is sick," he said solemnly.

"Sick?" she repeated, so alarmed that she dropped her fork. "What's the matter with him? Has he seen a doctor?"

Charlie shook his head, "You know Jake. He's stubborn as a mule. If I suggested he should go to a doctor, he would bite my head off and tell me to mind my own business."

"Oh, dear. What can we do?"

"Katie, you could go see him. He would talk to you," he replied urgently. "And you're a nurse. You'd know what's the matter with him."

"Well, I'm off for the next two days. Shall I come in the morning?"

"Could you come tonight?" He looked at her hopefully.

"Is it that bad?"

He nodded.

"Then I'll leave right after my shift ends at three. It won't take me long to be ready. There's already gas in the car," she said.

Kate nibbled at her sandwich and ate the fruit she had on her plate. She told him that Jake had written and asked if she wanted to go along when they gathered the cattle off the forest. He smiled and said, "I'm glad. We can use another hand and I hear you're quite a cowgirl."

She asked about Buster and Dickie . . . "and Jerry," she added remembering how he curled up on her lap at every opportunity. Charlie said that Dickie didn't come when he called. "You're his only human friend." Charlie told her he had a couple of errands to run then had to be on his way home.

Outside the cafeteria, Kate asked, "Will you tell Jake I'm coming? I don't want to upset him."

"No, I think it's best if I don't tell him. He wouldn't like me tattling on him. Just tell him you missed us." He grinned and gave her a warm hug. He held her by the shoulders and pleaded, "Honey, please help him get better. I really am worried."

She bit her lip and tried to blink back the tears that threatened. She stood a moment and watched Charlie walking down the corridor. He looked at his watch as he walked along.

———•———

When he reached home, Charlie watched for Jake and consulted his watch for the umpteenth time until he saw him coming in from the barn.

"You're home in good time. Did you get everything on the list?" Jake asked absently.

"Yes, got it all. I decided to go to Jackson and do the shopping there."

Jake turned sharply and asked, "Did you see Kate?"

Charlie sat at the table looking at his hands with a worried look on his face.

Jake sat down and said, "What's the matter?"

"She's sick, Jake. Real sick."

"She's sick?" Jake repeated anxiously. "Is she in the hospital?"

"That's where I found her." He worked his hands nervously and then looked up at Jake with imploring eyes, "Jake, I think you had better go see her . . . tonight," he added.

Jake stood up. "I guess you'll do the chores?" Jake said distractedly.

"Sure," Charlie replied as Jake left the room. Charlie looked at his watch again.

Several minutes later he stood at the front window and watched Kate's Buick come up the lane. He met her on the porch and led her into the dining room. "Wait here, I'll tell him you're here." He disappeared through the kitchen and she guessed that Jake must be in his room in bed. *That means he's sick*, she thought, knowing that Jake had to be pretty bad if he was in bed in the daytime.

In the bedroom where Jake was putting on a sweater after he had bathed and dressed, Charlie said, "There's someone here to see you."

"You talk to 'im. I'm leaving as soon as I get this bag packed."

Kate turned from where she'd been looking out toward the barn when she heard Charlie come back in the room. Before she could ask anything he said, "He'll be out in a minute. Do you want to sit down?" She shook her head no so he sat down himself where he had a mug of tea in front of him.

They both turned when they heard Jake coming through the kitchen. In the doorway he stopped and exclaimed, "Kate!" He dropped the suitcase and moved to stand in front of her where he looked for signs of her illness. "What are you doing here?"

A puzzled look spread over her face but she answered honestly, "I came to see you. You don't look sick."

"Who told you I'm sick?" Jake asked as he cast a suspicious glance at Charlie, who sat at the table watching the exchange wide-eyed.

"Where are you going with that suitcase?" she asked.

"Charlie told me that you were in the hospital sick, real sick. I was going to see you."

They both stared at Charlie. He held up both hands, palms out, and calmly said, "I didn't lie to either of you. I have never seen two people as lovesick as you two are."

Kate and Jake looked at each other and burst out laughing. He asked, "Are you lovesick?"

"Yes, I am. Are you lovesick?"

He nodded firmly. "Yes, I am!"

She asked tentatively, "Is that proposal still open?"

"Yes, ma'am, it certainly is."

"Then the answer is yes!" He caught her up and kissed her hard. She heard Charlie's chair scoot back. She pulled away then turned toward Charlie who had just gotten up from the table and was about to leave the room.

"Just one minute, Charlie," she said sternly. She pulled Jake along as she walked over to the older man.

She held his gaze as she said, "Charlie, you told me you wished you had a daughter like me. Well, I will be your daughter if you will be my father and walk me down the aisle to marry Jake."

Charlie's eyes filled with tears and his lower lip quivered. He couldn't say anything. Kate put her arms around him and hugged him tight. "Thank you," she whispered.

Jake clapped Charlie on the shoulder and shook his hand. "Lovesick, huh?" he chuckled. "Thanks, ol' man."

They watched him go and then Jake pulled Kate into his arms. "Can you believe what just happened?" he said, shaking his head.

Suddenly she said, as her hands smoothed the soft wool covering his chest, "You're wearing your sweater."

"Oh, yes, it was given to me by the lady I love." He covered her hands with his own.

"That's nice," she said with a wide smile. "I happen to know that the lady who gave it to you loves you too."

He kissed her gently then smiled down at her. "You'll have to live in the Bunkhouse, you know."

"I know," she said with a contented sigh. She snuggled closer while he slipped his hand into the soft shiny hair cascading down her back.

THE END

ACKNOWLEDGEMENTS

I will always be grateful to the people who helped bring this story to its conclusion.

My heartfelt gratitude goes to Gail Kearns for editing and guiding me through the process of publishing my novel, and to Sue Sommers at WRWS Design for the book design, illustrations, and production.

To Susan Lehr and Father Robert Lynch, S. J., thank you for proofreading the manuscript.

Thank you to my dear brother Donny Marincic for the cover artwork and creating a web site.

For factual information, I wish to thank Dr. William T. Close, Deanne Bradley, Lynn Thomas, Kevin Campbell, Gerry Endecott, Lance and Nila Hill, and Jonita Sommers.

I also appreciate the wonderful support and encouragement from my friends and family.

And lastly, I thank Eric Marincic for use of the Marincic family brand in the publishing house logo.

Helena Linn

ORDER FORM

To order additional copies of **Winter in the Bunkhouse** by Helena Linn, please fill out this form:

Name _____

Mailing Address

_____

_____

_____

Telephone _____

E-mail _____

Winter in the Bunkhouse

_____ copies x $22.95   _____

Subtotal   _____

Shipping and handling $5.00

Total $ _____

Mail with your check or money order to:

Seven Cross Lazy L Productions
P.O. Box 308
Big Piney, WY 83113, USA

For more information, email helenal@tribcsp.com
or visit http://7cross.marincic.com.